# LAST MAN ALIVE

A classic British murder mystery

JOHN DEAN

THE BOOK FOLKS

Published by The Book Folks

London, 2021



This book is a work of fiction. Names, characters, businesses, organizations, places and events are either the product of the author's imagination or are used fictitiously. Any resemblance to actual persons, living or dead, events or locales is entirely coincidental.



ISBN 978-1-913516-26-0

www.thebookfolks.com

*LAST MAN ALIVE is the ninth book by John Dean to feature DCI Jack Harris. It can be enjoyed as a stand-alone or as part of the series. Details of the other books are available at the end of this one.*

# Prologue

The midday sky was darkening above the northern hills as the man walked towards his tent, which he had erected at the base of the escarpment's sheer rock face the previous evening. He shivered as the chill wind rippled across the wind-blown moor, a herald of the storm due to sweep the North Pennines that afternoon. He pulled his coat tighter around him; a wiry, lean-faced man with little excess fat, he had always felt the cold, ever since he was a child.

Arriving at the camp, he busied himself with heating up his tinned stew on the stove. After that, he'd have no option but to sit the storm out. Once the food was ready, he retreated to the back of his tent, hacking into his loaf of bread with a knife while considering in gloomy silence the events of the morning. It had taken him more than a year to track his man down but he had finally managed it. Although he had only caught a brief glimpse through binoculars of a figure standing in the front window of Hillview Cottage, it had been enough to know that it was him. He had slipped his binoculars back into his rucksack and made his way down the slope to the cottage with a rising sense of anticipation. This was the culmination of all that work.

It had turned out to be a dispiriting encounter, though. The conversation that he had rehearsed in his mind a thousand times over recent months had not gone to plan and he had not even been granted entry to the cottage. After arguing on the doorstep for half an hour, he had left the cottage, promising to return the following day in the hope that things would be better. He returned to his campsite in sombre mood but the clamour of the gathering wind meant that he did not hear the intruder's approach until it was too late, the tent flap had been opened and the gun was pointing at him. The camper tried to stay calm as he looked at the new arrival and gestured towards the firearm.

'Is there really any need for that?' he said.

'I need to make sure that you agree not to tell the story. I assume he's at Hillview Cottage?'

'I'm saying nothing.'

'You don't have to,' said the gunman. 'It's the only place for miles around on the map. What did he tell you?'

'That's between him and me.' The camper gestured to the gun. 'For God's sake, will you put the bloody thing down so that we can discuss this sensibly!'

'I can't.'

'How about I agree to give you a cut of the–'

'This was never about money. You know that.' The gunman levelled the weapon at him. 'Now, I ask again, what did he say?'

'I'm saying nothing.' The camper pointed to the gun again. 'And I won't until you put that thing down.'

'From where I'm sitting, you have little option and–'

With a sudden move, the camper grabbed for his knife and lunged at the startled gunman. They grappled for a few seconds then the gunman twisted his weapon upwards until the barrel was a couple of centimetres from his opponent's face. The sound of the shot was lost in the rising shriek of the storm.

Back at Hillview Cottage, a lone figure slipped out of the house and disappeared into the rain-swept gloom without a backward glance.

# Chapter one

Since you are reading this, I must assume that I was not the last man alive, after all. I must also assume that you have found my body. That, in itself, is remarkable. I have always rather taken it for granted that no one would find me after I died. No one ever comes here and, recently, I had begun to believe that there was no one left alive anyway – that the human race had finally done what it always threatened to do and destroyed itself, whether by war or pestilence. I am also rather assuming that this letter is being read. Maybe it's not. Maybe it's mouldering away. Words speaking to nobody.

I am not sure when things changed. I say 'things changed' but I am not really sure that they did. Perhaps nothing 'happened'. Maybe my mind has played isolation's final trick. Maybe all of this is imagined. To be honest, I have struggled to differentiate reality from the imagined in recent months. Dementia – if that is what is afflicting me, and I have not consulted a doctor – can do that to you and isolation does not help. Things have certainly been getting worse over recent months.

If you are reading this, you can see that my home stands eight miles from the main road and is reached only by a rough track, inaccessible to all but the most robust of vehicles. When I moved here all those years ago, the removals van snapped an axle on the track and the men insisted that only the barest essentials could be transported to the house, which explains why it's so sparsely furnished. I didn't object – I came here to escape my old life. I was an advertising executive, one of those flash men who wore braces to the office and lived in an apartment in the middle of London, all ornaments and original paintings, the trappings of a well-paid lifestyle, and outside the sounds of a busy city. Today, here in my cottage, there's no noise. No television, no radio, no internet. Just the voices in my head. They are noise enough but I cannot seem to silence them. God knows, I have tried.

My isolation explains why it took so long to realise that something had happened. Even though no one ever visits me (I never receive post) I did have the occasional reminder that life goes on, usually in the form of hikers. Several weeks ago, or maybe months – I have little sense of time these days – there was a wildlife photographer. I assume he was a wildlife photographer; he had a camera and seemed interested in the ravens that nest on the escarpment, which is where he pitched his tent. Next morning, he had gone, leaving Haggs Scarr to the birds once more. Also reminding me about the outside world was the occasional drumming of engines over on the valley road. It was the cars that first made me realise that something had changed. I was cutting wood for the fire one day when I realised that I had not heard an engine for a long time. What if I was the last man alive? If it was true, it would mean I had finally attained everything I had always wanted. However, I must find out to be sure…

'And it just stops, does it?' asked Jack Harris. The detective chief inspector looked up from the pieces of paper in his hand then at the two officers standing in the living room of Hillview Cottage. 'There aren't any more pages?'

'No, that's it,' said Detective Sergeant Matty Gallagher. 'And what there is of it doesn't really make any sense.'

Harris did not reply. Not normally a prosaic man, the inspector was assailed by an overwhelming conviction that something had happened in the cottage. Something bad. And yet, as he glanced around the room, there was so sign of anything untoward, no overturned furniture, no blood smears, no nothing. Just a cottage that looked like it had been abandoned in a hurry. Letter left unfinished, front door unlocked.

'So, where is he?' he asked after a few moments' contemplation. He looked down at the two pages. 'Where's our author?'

'And *who* is he?' said Gallagher. 'There's no name on it.'

Harris scanned the neat handwriting again then looked round the room, which was sparsely furnished with a cream sofa and armchair, a magazine rack and a mahogany side table on the top of which until recently, he assumed, had sat a television. There were two paintings on the wall, a crudely-depicted forest scene in a selection of browns and a more colourful image of a young girl sitting at a window, reading a book.

'In fact, it's all pretty impersonal,' he said.

'It's the same in the other rooms,' said the third officer, a young woman with short blonde hair who was wearing a dark suit. 'The last man alive and we don't know who he is. Kinda ironic.'

'And there's nothing on the electoral register, you say?'

'Nothing,' said Detective Constable Alison Butterfield. 'According to the council, whoever lives here does not exist. Their records suggest this place has not been occupied since the elderly couple who lived here went into a home. That was three years ago.'

'Well, *someone's* been living here,' said Gallagher. He walked over to the magazine rack and removed a glossy nature publication, with a picture of a red squirrel on the cover. 'This is dated last month.'

'Intriguing,' said Harris. 'Mind, I have to say I quite like the idea of being the last man alive. It does have a certain appeal.'

His colleagues exchanged grins. Everyone knew that Jack Harris preferred animal to human company. Indeed, his dogs were sitting in the back of his white Land Rover, which was parked outside the cottage. Harris replaced the letter on the side table, sat down on the sofa and looked at Butterfield.

'Tell me again about our burglar, will you?' he said.

'Tommy Lacey,' she said. 'Traffic stopped his car in the early hours of this morning when he was on his way home to Lancashire. One of his headlights was out.'

'And he told us that he'd burgled this place?'

'He did, yes,' said Butterfield. 'According to Lacey, he reckoned the bad weather would mean there was less chance of him being heard as he broke in. Hillview Cottage was one of three houses he turned over last night. The other two were further up the valley road and the traffic guys found the stolen gear in the boot of his car. DVD players, laptops from the other places, a television from here. I've already been to take statements from the other owners. They didn't even know they'd been burgled. If it wasn't for his headlight, he'd have got away with it.'

'And we know him of old, I think?'

'From last year. He did nine houses over four nights down Carlisle way and one on the southern edge of our patch. It was tacked on as a TIC when Carlisle's case came to court. Lacey got six months. He's not long been out.'

'So why risk coming back?' asked Harris.

'He said he'd been told by someone in prison that there are rich pickings further up the valley.'

'A familiar story,' said Harris. 'Too familiar. Did Lacey say why he chose this cottage, in particular?'

'He hadn't planned to, but saw the lights from the road and found the place unlocked and deserted. I dropped in on my way back from visiting the other places.' Butterfield nodded at the handwritten sheets on the side table. 'That was so weird that I rang the sarge.'

'Weird is not the word,' said Gallagher. 'I mean, it doesn't fit with this place at all, does it? For a start, it's not eight miles from the main road like he says, more like two and hundred fifty metres. And he says he has no connection with the outside world, yet he had a telly and magazines. What's more, there's a phone socket and an Internet connection point as well.'

'If he has dementia, he probably got confused,' said Butterfield.

'*If* he has dementia,' said Harris. He gestured at the letter. 'I mean, could someone with dementia really write that?'

'It's possible,' said Gallagher. He noticed the inspector's sceptical expression. 'My father died with dementia. He hadn't a clue where he was half the time, but there were some times when you'd swear that there was nothing wrong with him. No, it all rings true to me.'

The sergeant shook his head.

'In fact, I have to admit that it's got me a little uneasy,' he said. 'The idea of him stuck up here on his own, slowly going out of his mind. It was bad enough with my dad when he was surrounded by people but to go through it all on your own... It just doesn't bear thinking about.'

'It is kinda spooky,' said Butterfield. She looked at Harris. 'So, where is he, do you think? Dead? Alive? Wandering the hills?'

'If the letter's genuine, my guess is that he's on the hills somewhere. We'll get Forensics to bear it in mind when they do their examination. Make sure we're not missing anything.' Harris gave them a sharp look. 'And I don't want any more talk about this place being spooky, either. That doesn't help anyone.'

The inspector walked over to the window and stared out at the ravine that stretched out above the cottage. The sky was clear and blue, the storm of the previous day having long since blown itself out, and he spent a few moments taking in the thinly scattered trees that hugged the banks of the fast-flowing stream, its waters full and bright and twisting following a week of storms. Harris turned back into the room.

'I'm sure that there's a perfectly rational explanation for this,' he said.

However, when Gallagher and Butterfield recalled the comment later in the day, neither of them sensed that the inspector sounded as if he was convinced.

# Chapter two

Forensics officer Kevin Guthrie shivered as he completed his examination of the living room amid the chill atmosphere of Hillview Cottage. He walked through to the kitchen, where his colleague was dusting the table for fingerprints.

'You nearly finished?' he asked. He hoped that she would say yes. There was something about the cottage that was unsettling, even though neither of them had found evidence to indicate that anything was amiss.

'This is my last job,' said Mary Josephs.

'Anything?'

'Not really. You?'

'Just the prints that Tommy Lacey left when he burgled the place,' said Guthrie. 'And those partials you found upstairs, although I don't hold out much hope for them, mind. They look too fragmented to me.'

Josephs finished her examination of the table-top.

'If you ask me,' she said, 'this guy knew what he was doing. The place has been wiped clean of prints. What about the outside?'

'There's the odd boot-print but nothing you can really identify after all that rain. I take it we're good to go then?'

'Give me a couple of minutes,' said Josephs. She started to pack her equipment away.

'No longer,' said Guthrie.

He walked back into the living room where he stood at the window for a few moments and watched a couple of mud-spattered uniformed police officers who, having searched the area around the cottage, were getting into their patrol car. Guthrie opened the window and grimaced as the chill wind rushed in from the hillside.

'Anything interesting?' he yelled.

'Nothing,' replied one of the uniforms as he climbed into the passenger seat. 'It would help if we knew what we were looking for. The light's going now so we're off anyway.'

Guthrie closed the window and watched the vehicle bump its way back down the track towards the main road. He turned back into the living room and reached into his pocket for the front door key, which he had found while searching a drawer. Josephs emerged from the kitchen.

'All done,' she said.

'Matty Gallagher's right about this place giving you the willies,' said Guthrie. She shivered. The temperature in the cottage had dipped sharply since he had opened the window.

'Better not let Jack Harris hear you saying that. He's banned that kind of talk, apparently.'

'Yes, well he's not here, is he?' said Guthrie. 'Come on, let's get out of here.'

They walked outside and slipped out of their white overalls. Guthrie locked the front door, pinned up the note giving contact details should anyone return to the cottage, and they got into their car. As they did so, both officers had an overwhelming sense that they were being watched. Instinctively, they glanced over to the cottage, half-expecting to see someone standing in the living room window. There was no one there. Guthrie shivered again, slipped the car into gear and headed down the track.

* * *

Eleven miles to the south of Hillview Cottage, in the hillside market town of Levton Bridge, Jack Harris was experiencing unsettling thoughts of his own as he sat in his first-floor office and sifted through reports from his team about the cottage.

'It doesn't make sense,' he said to his dogs, Scoot and Archie – mongrels both – curled up next to the radiator.

Harris placed the reports back on his desk, sighed and stared out of the window, where the first glow was emanating from the street lamps that were ranged along the road which led past the Victorian police station and continued up the hill towards the marketplace.

There was a knock on the door and Harris smiled a welcome as Matty Gallagher entered the room. They were very different men, Harris, born and bred in the valley, at home on the hills, strong-jawed and with thick brown hair without a hint of grey, Gallagher, a decade younger, smaller, stocky, black hair starting to thin, a man, some said, with the appearance of a monk, a Londoner who had left his job with the Metropolitan Police and moved to the area so that his wife could be nearer her elderly parents. Harris nodded at the documents on his desk.

'We don't seem to be much further forward, Matty lad,' he said. '*Someone* must know who the guy at the cottage is.'

'You've seen the reports. The postman has delivered magazines to Hillview Cottage for the past year, but has never seen anyone. No one at the shops in the nearest villages knows who lives there, Lacey insists the place was empty when he screwed it and none of the area's doctors have a record of a patient living at the address.'

'We must have found *something* to say who he is.' Harris tossed the pieces of paper back onto the desk in exasperation. 'I mean, nobody is anonymous in this day and age, surely? I can't switch on my mobile phone without some bastard texting me about double glazing. It's like they know I live half-way up a hillside.'

'They probably do,' said Gallagher. 'Besides, we do know something. We've got plenty of names for him. It's just that we don't think any of them are genuine. He gave a different one to everyone with whom he dealt, including the utilities and the wildlife magazine publisher when he took out the subscription. And he had a load of different bank accounts. As far as we can work out from putting it all together, he moved in just over six months ago.' The sergeant shook his head. 'And he's been there ever since, losing his mind.'

'Unless he was faking it.'

'Why would you think that?' asked Gallagher.

'Well, surely, someone with dementia couldn't do all of that?'

Before Gallagher could reply, Alison Butterfield appeared at the office door.

'We've had a sighting,' said the detective constable.

'Really?' replied Harris. 'Recent?'

Her face clouded over.

'Ah, well, there's the hitch,' she said. 'It happened the best part of three months ago.'

'It's a start,' said Harris. 'Who saw him?'

'The Tesco driver who delivers stuff to the cottage. He usually leaves it in the outhouse as instructed but, on this occasion, he caught sight of a man standing in the front window. Short grey hair and wearing a blue sweater. He reckons he was in his seventies. The man stepped back into the room when he realised that he had been clocked, and the driver hasn't seen him since.'

'Well, at least we know that he's real,' said Harris. 'Do Tesco have a name?'

'The account was set up by Matthew Rider but we reckon it's another fake.' Butterfield glanced at Gallagher. 'That's right, isn't it, Sarge?'

Gallagher nodded. Harris thought for a few moments.

'OK,' he said. 'Let's assume that the letter is a hoax. Is there a chance that we could be looking at a professional?

He clearly knows how to conceal his real identity and Forensics say that he left precious little for them to go on. Maybe the letter is designed to confuse us.'

'Well, it worked,' said Gallagher.

'At least we know what he looks like now,' said Harris. 'Good work, Alison.'

Butterfield nodded her appreciation; as one of the department's younger officers and keen to make an impression, she valued the praise and was smiling broadly as she walked back into the corridor just as a slim, balding uniformed officer approached. Philip Curtis, the Divisional Commander, nodded at her and continued on to the inspector's office, where he scowled as he noticed the dogs slumbering beneath the radiator. Although he and Harris had worked hard to develop a working relationship following a difficult start to the commander's tenure at Levton Bridge, the presence of the dogs at the station remained one of their disagreements. However, they were popular with the rest of the staff so, as usual, Curtis said nothing. Besides, he had other things on his mind. Gallagher made as if to leave the room, but Curtis motioned for him to stay seated.

'Problem?' asked Harris.

'I was just wondering about this man at Hillview Cottage,' said Curtis. 'We seem to be devoting quite a bit of time to it. Are we any further forward?'

'Not really,' said Harris.

'Well, just so long as we do not allow it to distract us from other things.' Curtis tried to sound casual. Unconcerned. As if the thought had only just occurred to him. Experience had taught him that it was the best way to avoid triggering the inspector's stubborn streak. 'I mean, there's plenty else to be going on with, isn't there? Those quad bike thefts down at Enderby, for example. I'm coming under a lot of pressure from the local councillors and *The Herald* is going to run a piece this week. Isn't it most likely that a relative became concerned about the state of mind of the guy at the cottage and came to take him away?'

'Ordinarily, I would have agreed with you,' said Harris. 'But would someone that caring go without locking the front door and leaving the key behind? Look, I know that there's probably a perfectly rational explanation, but it feels wrong leaving things as they are.'

'So, what's the plan?' asked Curtis.

'The mountain rescue guys are due to do a training day tomorrow – they've got a couple of new members – and I've persuaded them to switch it to the area around Hillview Cottage. See if they can turn up anything.'

'As long as they know that it could turn out to be a wild goose chase,' said the commander. He looked at Gallagher. 'What do you think, Sergeant?'

'I think it's worth a try,' said the sergeant. 'After all, how hard can it be to find the last man alive?'

# Chapter three

'Any idea which direction he might have gone?' asked Bob Crowther. The leader of the mountain rescue team looked at Harris as they stood outside Hillview Cottage early the next morning. 'Assuming that he's up here, of course.'

'And that's a big assumption,' said Harris.

The two old friends were silent for a few moments as they stared out across hills that were dappled with shadows cast by the autumn sun. Harris's dogs sat in eager anticipation of the walk to come while, a few metres away, the remaining members of the mountain rescue team decamped from their minibus, climbed into their waterproofs and prepared their haversacks.

'Are you still going with us?' asked Crowther.

'For a couple of hours,' said the inspector. 'I'm not sure that I'll get away with more than that. My commander is already a bit twitchy about the amount of effort that we're expending on this one.'

'But if there's a chance that he *is* up here…' said Crowther.

He did not finish the sentence. He did not need to. North Country born and bred, both men appreciated the dangers presented by the Pennine landscape. Harris had spent his childhood roaming the hills with a dog at his heels until he left to join the Army as a teenager. Having returned to the UK to work as a police officer in Manchester, the siren call of the hills had eventually brought him home to the valley, as he always knew that it would, and his first decision on arriving in Levton Bridge had been to volunteer to join the mountain rescue team.

Standing a few metres away, Crowther's deputy, Mike Ganton, completed his preparations, checked that the rest of the team were ready, shouldered his bag and walked over to Harris and Crowther.

'We're good to go,' he said. 'What's the thinking, fellas?

'Well, if he's an old-ish fellow, he won't have gone far,' said Crowther. 'And he's likely to have kept to the main walking trails, I would guess. What do you reckon, Hawk?'

'Not sure,' said Harris. '*If* he is suffering from dementia, he might easily have strayed off the path. Become confused and fallen or simply just lain down and gone to sleep. Succumbed to hypothermia. He could be anywhere, but he does mention Haggs Scarr in his letter so that would be a decent place to aim for.'

'It's as good place as any,' said Crowther. He slipped on his backpack and glanced at the inspector's dogs. 'Hopefully, the boys can sniff something out. Come on, let's get on with it. There's another spell of bad weather due to come in by late afternoon and we want to avoid that, if we can.'

For the next hour, the team walked with steady and sure foot and, once at the summit of the nearest hill, Crowther paused to lift his binoculars to his eyes and scan the landscape. He pointed west along a ridge and the team walked for another half an hour before dropping down onto heather moorland, where they reached a rocky outcrop and Crowther called a halt. Flasks of coffee and chocolate bars were produced from rucksacks and Harris reached into his bag for treats for the dogs, who watched him eagerly. Crowther sipped at his coffee and chewed on a Mars bar as he stared across the moor towards the towering sheer cliff face of Haggs Scarr in the distance.

'Not sure how much more time we can give this once we get to the escarpment, Hawk,' he said. 'We really will have to crack on with our ropes training before the weather closes in.'

'I agree,' said Ganton, who was sitting nearby. 'We could search for hours and not find your guy. I mean, we don't even know that he's up here, do we?'

'A wild goose chase was the phrase my commander used,' said the inspector.

'Maybe he's right,' said Ganton. 'Let's be honest, we're only doing it to say that we tried, aren't we?'

'I guess so.' Harris glanced at his watch. 'And I'll have to get back soon, anyway. Curtis will go spare if I'm out all day.'

The raucous call of a raven attracted their attention. Harris, a keen birdwatcher part of whose job was as force wildlife liaison officer for the area, lifted his binoculars and focused on the bird as it flew towards the escarpment.

'First raven I've seen at Haggs Scarr for a while,' he said. 'There used to be a breeding pair up on the top but I thought that they had... hang on, what's that?'

Crowther and Ganton lifted their binoculars and followed his gaze towards the base of the escarpment.

'It appears to be a tent,' said Crowther. He focused in closer and frowned. 'And something about it doesn't look right.'

'It looks like it might have been abandoned,' said Ganton. He glanced at Harris. 'Next time I question your judgement when it comes to wild geese, tell me to shut up.'

Harris gave a slight smile but it was quickly replaced by an expression of concern as he continued to survey the campsite through his binoculars. As he did so, the inspector experienced the same sensations he had experienced in Hillview Cottage the previous day, the sensation for which he had rebuked colleagues. The sensation that something was badly wrong. Harris thought back to the letter which was now nestling in the top drawer of his office and, as he did so, he felt a knot forming in the pit of his stomach.

* * *

Detective Sergeant Charlie Bourne was sitting in his first-floor office at force headquarters, sipping from his mug of tea as he caught up on his intelligence reports after a few days off. He looked at the long list of emails in his inbox and shook his head; it had only been a long weekend with his wife and the children but already there were dozens of them, all demanding to be read and all wasting his time. He was relieved when the desk phone rang and he was able to focus on something else.

'DS Bourne?' said a woman's voice. 'This is Switchboard. We've got a police officer on the line from Germany who says that he wants to speak to someone from Special Branch. Can you take the call?'

'Sure,' said Bourne. 'Put him through.'

There was a click on the line.

'Hello, am I speaking to Detective Sergeant Bourne?' said a cultured voice.

'You are, yes.'

'I am Josef Haller, an intelligence officer with the German Police, based in Dusseldorf.' The English was impeccable and delivered with only the slightest hint of a German accent. 'I require your help on a somewhat delicate matter. Do you know a man called Kevin Guthrie?'

'Guthrie?' said Bourne. He thought for a few moments. 'Yes, I think that he's one of our forensics people. Why would the German police be interested in him?'

'I take it that this conversation is confidential?' said Haller. There was an edge to the voice now. 'I would hate for this matter to become common knowledge.'

'You have my word,' said Bourne. He was intrigued by the call. 'Has Kevin done something wrong?'

'Let's just say that he is taking an interest in someone about whom we would rather he did not ask questions,' said Haller. 'I would like you to find out why he is so interested in this individual and instruct him to cease his inquiries immediately.'

'Hang on, I'm not sure I can–'

'If you find yourself unable to comply with the request, I am authorised to take it to your chief constable,' said Haller.

'There's no need to get heavy.'

'My apologies. However, your Mr Guthrie has stumbled on something of the utmost sensitivity, a matter of national security for both our countries and I cannot afford our inquiries to be jeopardised...'

* * *

Back on the hills, Jack Harris and the mountain rescue team were walking towards the escarpment when they heard the distant clatter of rotor blades and watched as a helicopter appeared on the western horizon and flew low over the hills towards them. The inspector's mobile rang.

'Hi, Jack,' said a voice that he recognised as Mark Ramage, air crew with the National Police Air Service. 'We're on our way back from a job and heard you might need some help.'

'Much appreciated,' said Harris. 'What was the job?'

'An old dear out walking her dog disappeared over by Scarpton Lake. Turns out that she'd taken a header into the water.'

'Is the dog OK?' asked Harris.

'You never change, do you?' chuckled Ramage. 'Yeah, the dog's fine. Not so sure about the old dear, though. Anyway, we've got thirty minutes flying time before we have to head back to refuel. Where do you want us to look?'

'We've seen a tent over by the escarpment.'

'Yeah, we've just seen it, too,' said Ramage. 'We'll go and have a look-see.'

As the aircraft swooped in low towards Haggs Scarr, the mountain rescue team headed for the site as quickly as they could. There was a fresh urgency about their tread now, each team member filled with a sense of trepidation at what they might find. The helicopter reached the escarpment first and the pilot took great care to keep the rotor blades clear of the sheer rock wall as the aircraft hovered above the tent. The inspector's mobile phone rang again.

'Any sign of life?' asked Harris.

'Looks like it's been abandoned,' said Ramage. 'We'll take a look round the rest of the area, see what we can find.'

'Cheers.'

As the helicopter veered away and began to criss-cross the hillside, the search team arrived at the base of the escarpment and made their way to the tent. Crowther and Harris stood in silence as they glimpsed a shape through the open flap.

'I have this awful feeling,' said Crowther.

Harris peered into the tent, only to give a slight cry and recoil at the sight of a dead man lying on his back, his mangled facial features obscured by torn flesh and blood. Hand over his nose, the inspector emerged into the fresh air and began to retch. Crowther brushed past him and, wrinkling his nose to counter the smell of death, bent down to take a closer look. He looked into the sightless eyes staring up out of the mess, crawled back out and crouched low to the ground for a few moments. He looked at Harris.

'Definitely not your guy,' he said. 'He looks much younger.'

Harris nodded and glanced over to where the rest of the mountain rescue team had gathered in silence.

'Stay back, please, guys,' he said. 'This has just become a crime scene.'

The inspector's mobile phone rang again.

'You find anything?' asked Ramage.

'Too much,' said Harris. 'One dead. Shot in the face. What about you?'

'There's a copse about a mile due east of where you are standing,' said Ramage. 'It's on a track that leads to the C road. There's a vehicle in among the trees. Looks like it's been torched. We're running short of fuel so we're going to have to turn for home. Let Control know if you need us to come back out and assist you further.'

'Yeah, will do,' said Harris. 'Thanks, Mark. Talk later.'

'Later, dude,' said Ramage.

As the helicopter peeled away, Harris took a moment to gather his thoughts; the mysterious man in Hillview Cottage had transformed from potential victim to possible suspect. The inspector scanned through the contact list on his mobile phone and punched in the number for Gillian Roberts, Levton Bridge's detective inspector, the organiser, the best person to have by your side in an emergency.

'Gillian,' he said. 'We've found a body at Haggs Scarr. Looks like a murder so we'll need to set up the whole kit and kaboodle. Can you handle it?'

'Sure.'

'Be warned, it'll be a complicated one to organise.'

'Complicated is not the word,' said Roberts.

'What does that mean?'

'I've got Kevin Guthrie from Forensics here. I'll let him explain. Damned if I can.'

'Hello, sir,' said Guthrie. 'I thought you'd like to know that a weird thing happened when I tried to check the partial fingerprints that we found yesterday at Hillview Cottage. I came up with nothing on the UK database so I checked the European records. Dotting the Is and crossing the Ts, really. Didn't expect to find anything but it turns out that our prints could be a match with a record that is classified.'

'By whom?' asked Harris.

'I don't know. It wouldn't let me in.'

'Any way you can override it?'

'I don't have that kind of authority, I am afraid,' said Guthrie. 'I asked my governor if she could find a way round it but she's locked out, too. Whoever put the record in there doesn't want anyone seeing the information without their say-so.'

'Put Gillian back on, will you?'

'Hi,' said Roberts. 'Intriguing, eh? So, this body? Do we know– Hello, to what do we owe the honour of your presence among us humble mortals?'

Harris could sense the surprise in her voice as she conducted a conversation with a man. 'What's happening?' he asked.

It was a man's voice which answered. 'Hello, Jack.'

'Charlie Bourne, is it?' said Harris.

'The very same.'

'And, pray, what are Special Branch doing cluttering up my nice, tidy CID squad room?'

'I'd rather not discuss it on the phone. Suffice to say that we have a shared interest in your man at Hillview Cottage and I'm guessing that extends to the body that you have just found as well. Can you get back to Levton Bridge to talk it over?'

Harris glanced at the tent.

'It's not exactly convenient,' he said.

'Then might I suggest that you make it convenient?' said Bourne.

## Chapter four

Things moved quickly following the discovery of the body as Gillian Roberts swung into action. Sitting with a mug of tea in his hand, Charlie Bourne could appreciate the energy as he watched officers listen to the detective inspector rattle off her instructions then scuttle off to carry out her bidding. It brought back memories of his time as a CID officer. If Bourne was honest, although he had found his level of access to top level information exciting following his move to Special Branch, there were times when he yearned for the day-to-day involvement of general policing. He gave a knowing smile as Roberts grabbed a few minutes to brew herself a tea, sat down at a nearby desk and closed her eyes for a few moments. She opened her eyes again and noticed his smile.

'And what's tickled your funny bone?' she asked.

'Takes me back,' said Bourne. He took a sip of his drink. 'Any idea when Jack will be here?'

'An hour, maybe. Maybe less. The chopper's going to bring him back when it takes Matty Gallagher and Kevin Guthrie up there. You going to tell me what this is all about then, Charlie?'

'I can't.'

'Can't or won't?'

'You know the rules, Gillian.' Bourne thought for a moment. 'What I can say is that it's a request from an outside force. We knew nothing about the existence of your bloke at the cottage until we were contacted this morning.'

'Which force rang you? And how come they are interested in our man?'

Bourne did not reply.

'Come on, Charlie,' said Roberts. 'You're not talking to an amateur here, you know. I remember you when you were a snot-nosed rookie not long out of diapers, remember. I won't tell anyone.'

'Like hell you won't.' Bourne was wary; he knew that the mother-of-two's carefully cultivated matronly demeanour masked a detective's mind as sharp as they came. 'Nice try, though.'

'OK, I admit defeat.' Roberts held up her hands in mock surrender. 'But I'm not sure Jack Harris will. You know what he's like. Need-to-know is just about his least favourite phrase in the world.'

Bourne frowned; he was not looking forward to the confrontation with the chief inspector. Although the men had not worked together, he had heard all the stories and, having encountered Harris on a couple of in-house training courses at headquarters, had quickly realised that you only got as close to the inspector as he wanted you to. And also that you crossed him at your peril. The thought of the encounter to come filled him with foreboding.

'Yes,' he said with a sigh. 'I know what he's like.'

'Rather you than me,' said Roberts. The detective inspector took a sip of her chamomile tea and watched as a young woman with close-cropped dark hair entered the room. Roberts beckoned her over. 'Sally, just the person. I've got a little job for you.'

Constable Sally Orr walked over with an eager look on her face. As the CID department's newest and by far the youngest recruit, she relished being part of a major inquiry and was desperate to prove herself.

'What is it?' she asked.

'I've just sent Alison out with Forensics to check the burnt-out car in the copse,' said Roberts. 'Can you pick up her check of Misper records, please? If we're lucky, someone will have reported our man in the tent missing.'

* * *

The police helicopter landed a hundred metres from Haggs Scarr and Kevin Guthrie and Matty Gallagher jumped out and made their way over to the spot where Harris and the mountain rescue team were gathered. Guthrie gestured to the tent.

'He in there?' he said.

'Yeah, he is,' said Harris. 'Be warned, though, he's a right mess.'

'So I hear.'

Harris glanced at the gathering clouds.

'I know it's a crime scene, Kevin, but be as quick as you can, yeah?' he said. 'We need to get him off the hills before the weather closes in.'

'Will do,' said Guthrie. He donned his white overalls and disappeared into the tent with his equipment case only to re-emerge a couple of moments later, pale and with his eyes closed. Harris watched him retch.

'I told you,' said the inspector.

The forensics officer nodded weakly and, after taking a few moments to regain his composure, he went back into the tent.

'That bad, eh?' said Gallagher.

'That bad,' said Harris.

'I take it there's no ID on him?'

Harris shook his head.

'So, who do you think he is?' asked the sergeant. He glanced at the tent. 'Our man from Hillview Cottage?'

'He's too young.'

'So, he could be the wildlife photographer that he wrote about in the letter.'

'Who knows?' said Harris. 'But the presence of a Special Branch officer in our squad room would seem to suggest that there's more to this than some old guy suffering from dementia, Matty lad. Did you get a chance to talk to Charlie Bourne before you came away?'

'Much good did it do me. You know what these secret squirrel types are like, guv. The DI was trying the motherly approach as I was leaving. She was his sergeant when he started out in the job, apparently.'

'I'm not sure that even Gillian's motherly approach will work with Special Branch.' Harris tapped the side of his nose. 'Need-to-know, Matty lad, and, clearly, we humble CID types are not deemed important enough in the scheme of things.'

* * *

A mile to the east of Haggs Scarr, Alison Butterfield and forensics officer Mary Josephs stood in the copse and surveyed the remains of the burnt-out Vauxhall Astra. Whoever had set fire to the vehicle had done a thorough job. A further attempt to conceal the identity of the car had been made by the removal of the front and rear registration plates. The detective constable watched as Josephs peered into the melted remnants of the glove compartment.

'Anything?' asked Butterfield hopefully.

'Nothing,' said Josephs. She re-emerged from the interior of the vehicle. 'We'll not come up with any prints with all this fire damage, I don't think. It's like at the cottage. Someone has gone to a lot of trouble to cover their traces, Alison. Everything about this smacks of a professional.'

'Hence the interest being shown by Special Branch,' said Butterfield. 'Any idea how long the vehicle has been here?'

'Difficult to tell.' Josephs surveyed the area surrounding the car. 'There was definitely a second vehicle, mind. There's two sets of tyre tracks but they're not very distinct. Thin pickings, I am afraid.'

Butterfield phoned Harris.

'We're at the copse, guv,' she said. 'Forensics says there's virtually nothing of use here.'

'Yeah, same here,' said Harris. He glanced over to where Guthrie was on his knees, examining the ground around the tent. 'The DI has arranged for a recovery truck to come and take the car back to the garage for a more thorough examination. Let me know when it arrives, will you?'

Harris ended the call and stared in moody silence across the moor then back at the tent. Finally, he looked at the sergeant.

'What the hell is this about, Matty lad?' he said.

'Hopefully, Special Branch will enlighten us when we get back. Maybe the presence of a DCI will loosen their tongues.'

'It would be a first if it does.'

'Certainly would,' said Gallagher gloomily. The sergeant had encountered Special Branch officers on several occasions during his time with the Metropolitan Police and each incident had proved to be a frustrating experience. 'They do like to play things close to their chest.'

Kevin Guthrie concluded his examination of the site, stood up and walked over to them.

'Anything?' asked Harris.

'Nothing worth talking about.'

Bob Crowther heard the comment and walked over.

'Does that mean we can get back then?' he asked Harris. He glanced up at the darkening sky. 'The weather's closing in and the light will go early. I don't really fancy being stuck up here in a storm with a dead body.'

'Fine by me. If you get him to Hillview Cottage, Gillian has arranged for an ambulance to take him down to

Roxham General for the post-mortem. I'm going back to Levton Bridge in the chopper.'

'You're not coming with us?' asked Crowther.

'I've been summoned.'

'Who on earth is brave enough to summon you?' said Crowther. 'Or should I say, foolhardy?'

'Don't ask,' said Harris sourly.

Crowther turned to his team.

'Let's get him ready!' he shouted.

Harris tossed the Land Rover keys to Gallagher.

'Can you take it back to Levton Bridge for me, Matty lad?' he asked. 'It's parked outside the cottage. And take the dogs as well, will you?'

'No lovely ride back in the nice warm helicopter then?' said the sergeant wistfully.

'I am afraid not. We need a police officer to accompany the body.'

Gallagher dug his hands deep into his anorak pockets and stared out over hills which were looking ever bleaker as the clouds gathered.

'Now how did I know you were going to say that?' he said.

# Chapter five

Jack Harris sat behind his desk and tried to gauge the measure of Charlie Bourne. Although he had met the Special Branch officer before, the sergeant had not made much of an impression on him. Now, Harris tried to work out if Bourne was someone likely to wilt under the pressure of the inspector's tough stance or someone who needed a more nuanced approach. The fact that Bourne had felt confident enough to insist that the senior officer return to the police station despite the difference in rank suggested the latter – and Jack Harris was acutely aware that he did not do nuance particularly well. Or at all.

For his part, Bourne tried to look relaxed under the DCI's intense stare. He knew Harris's reputation as a man who brooked no obstruction when it came to furthering his inquiries and the inspector's body language suggested that there was no chance of him accepting vague replies now. He had not even offered the visitor a cup of tea. Bourne resolved to appear co-operative but was determined only to give the inspector the minimum amount of information.

'So,' said Harris. He, too, had decided to attempt a conciliatory approach to begin with. 'Are you going to tell me what this is all about, Charlie? I do hope so, because the last thing I want is for us to fall out over it. We're on the same side, when all's said and done.'

'I'll do what I can. However, I am sure you can appreciate that I am strictly limited in what I can say. It's on a need-to-know basis.'

Harris gave him a sharp look and Bourne cursed himself silently for being so glib. Kill me now, he thought.

'Listen, sunshine,' said Harris. His voice had an edge to it as he leaned forward in his chair. 'I have a John Doe who has been shot in the face and a missing man who may well have pulled the trigger and there's a good chance that you know the identity of both of them. If that's not a "need-to-know basis", then I am not sure what is.'

'Bad phraseology. I apologise.' Bourne tried to keep his voice steady; he'd heard the reports of the inspector's temper down the years, how it had, on occasion, spilled over into something more physical than just words. And not always with villains. 'However, I can assure you that I do not know the identity of your man in the tent or the guy who killed him.'

'I think you *do* know who the man is at Hillview Cottage and I think you also know why his fingerprints triggered an alert.'

Bourne did not reply.

'Look, Charlie,' said Harris. 'I need to wrap this one up as quickly as possible. You know what people are like in this area. They get panicky when someone steals a quad bike so you can imagine what the thought of a gunman roaming the hills will do to them when we release the news. And who can blame them? I'd be worried. I *am* worried. At least, give me something to go on.'

Again, Bourne hesitated.

'I am prepared to take this further if I have to,' said Harris. His patience was wearing thin. 'I don't wish to cause trouble for you but how do you think the chief constable will react when I tell him that his Special Branch people are withholding information from one of his own murder investigations? Particularly one that I imagine he would very much like wrapping up PDQ.'

'You're not the first person to threaten me with the chief constable today,' said Bourne bleakly.

'Presumably, the other person was the one who called you after Kevin triggered the alert on the fingerprints?'

Bourne nodded.

'Are you going to tell me who put the block on the record?' asked the inspector. 'Who contacted you, Charlie?'

'All I can say is that he is a police officer with a force based on the Continent.'

'It's a big continent.'

Harris picked up his desk phone.

'Now,' he murmured, 'I wonder if can remember the chief's extension number.'

'Germany.'

'Well, that's something at least. So, our man in Hillview Cottage is German?'

'English. He lived in Germany.'

'And his name?' asked Harris. He still held the telephone receiver in his hand.

'I can't give you that,' said Bourne. 'Suffice to say that he was involved in a police inquiry in Germany.'

'*Was* involved? When was this?'

Bourne did not reply. Harris glanced down at the phone keypad and reached out with his forefinger.

'Extension 276,' he said. 'Or is 277? I can never remember which.'

Bourne sighed.

'It happened in the mid-eighties,' he said.

'Before the Berlin Wall came down. Are we talking East or West Germany, Charlie?'

'West, but, like I said, our German friends would rather that you stay away from this. They regard it as a matter of national security and, from what I can see, you have nothing definite to link him with the murder anyway.'

Harris replaced the receiver on its cradle.

'That's true enough,' he said. 'But it's early days, which is why anything you can tell us is so important. Do you–'

'I'm sorry.' Bourne stood up. 'I've already told you more than I should have. Ring the chief constable if you want to make something of it but my governor will back me up, I am sure.'

'I'm sure she will,' said Harris. He watched as Bourne opened the door. 'We won't stop digging, though.'

'We'll see about that.'

Harris thought about remonstrating further with the sergeant but something about the Special Branch man's demeanour suggested that he had pushed it as far as he could go.

'Thanks anyway,' he said instead.

Bourne turned back to face the inspector with an apologetic look on his face.

'I wish I could tell you more,' he said. 'I really do.'

Once Bourne had gone, Harris picked up his desk phone and rang the detective inspector.

'Can you pop in, please, Gillian?' he said.

Sitting in her office, Roberts replaced the receiver and glanced up to see Charlie Bourne walking past her door. She waved at him, but he was engaged in an intense conversation on his mobile phone and did not appear to have noticed the gesture. A couple of minutes later, she was sitting in Harris's office, listening to the chief inspector's account of his conversation.

'Well, at least we've got *something* to go on now,' she said.

'I wondered if he might be part of a witness protection programme,' said Harris. 'It wouldn't be the first time that they've placed people like that in our area without telling us. Whoever he is, he must be pretty high level for people to go to all this trouble to protect him.'

'But after forty years?'

'Criminals have long memories,' said Harris. 'Of course, he may not be under witness protection. Maybe he's a villain on the run. Police officers have long memories, too.'

'Then why will the German police not take us into their confidence?'

'Maybe they want to arrest him before we do,' said Harris. 'Maybe it's a case of good old police politics.'

'I take it we're going to keep looking for an answer?'

'Until someone orders us not to,' said Harris. 'But we need to be careful. If it is something heavy, no one will thank us for blundering in. Can you get someone to do a desk search? See if we can track down anything on the Internet about an Englishman involved in crime in Germany in the mid-eighties. That can't do any harm.'

'I can do but intelligence gathering was very rudimentary in those days, remember. When I started in the job, a lot of the information was still stored on card indexes. It took ages to find anything.'

'How about the newspapers then?' asked Harris. 'Perhaps they reported on an Englishman who was in trouble with the German police? A court appearance, maybe?'

'Same issue. The information is likely to be on microfilm or hard copy, assuming that the archives still exist. A friend of mine works for a newspaper down south and half their archive was destroyed because no one ever went into the room where it was stored so no one knew that the roof was leaking. I'll get someone on it, though.'

As she left the office, Philip Curtis walked into the room. The commander glanced over to the radiator and gave a slight smile when he saw that the dogs were not there. Harris read his mind.

'They're on the way back down from Haggs Scarr,' he said.

'Ah,' said Curtis. The commander sat down and looked across the desk at Harris. 'You've been ruffling feathers again, Jack.'

'Don't tell me – Special Branch have been onto you?'

'Not to me,' said Curtis. 'I've had the chief constable on. He's just received a call from Charlie Bourne's boss. Not sure you've met her yet? DCI Janet Maynard. She's new. Came over from North Yorkshire three weeks ago.'

'Not yet, no,' said Harris.

'She's worried that Charlie told you more than he should have. She's concerned that we may jeopardise whatever it is that the Germans are up to.'

'Then perhaps they should tell us what it is,' said Harris. 'What did the chief tell her?'

'That you are to be allowed to get on with your investigation until someone comes up with a good reason not to, but you're to keep her in the loop. She's our point of contact from now on. Whatever this is about, Jack, it's big.'

* * *

The light was fading fast as the mountain rescue team carried the stretcher bearing the body the final few metres to Hillview Cottage and the waiting ambulance. Following in their tracks, Gallagher turned to look back along the route they had taken, which was already vanishing from view as the storm clouds descended and a sheet of rain began to fall over the tops. The sergeant glanced down at his mud-smeared trousers and sighed then watched as Crowther helped his team load the body into the ambulance. Once the job was done, Crowther placed his bag into the team's minibus and walked over.

'That's us,' he said.

'Thanks for turning out, Bob.'

'I'm just glad we found someone.' Crowther looked at the rain now sweeping its way down the slope towards them, glanced at the cottage and frowned. 'Do you think your guy is still out there somewhere?'

'God knows,' said Gallagher. He thought of his father's final days, beset as they had been by bewilderment and, in those moments when clarity forced its way to the surface, fear. 'I hope not, Bob, I really do.'

'The record's sixteen months.'

'Record?'

'To find someone. A chap in his seventies who went for a hike on his own. Silly really, wrong shoes, no waterproof and no mobile phone. We looked everywhere for him – took three days on it – but he only turned up the following year when a couple of walkers found him lying next to a stream.' Crowther watched his team as they packed their equipment into the minibus. 'Anyway, we'll be off.'

For reasons that neither man could rationalise, they both looked across at the cottage at the same time, overwhelmed by the sensation that someone was watching them and half expecting to see someone standing in the living room window. However, no one was there. Crowther gave the sergeant a troubled look.

'You know,' he said. 'I could have sworn–'

'Yeah, me, too,' said Gallagher. 'I tell you, this place gives me the creeps. Don't tell the governor, though. He has no time for talk like that.'

Crowther nodded, patted the sergeant on the shoulder and walked over to the minivan. Gallagher had just let the inspector's dogs into the back of the Land Rover when his mobile phone rang.

'Hiya, Matty,' said his wife's voice. 'Are you still looking for an expert who can help you with your weird letter?'

'Yeah. You got someone?'

'I asked a few of the other nurses and they suggested Professor Neal Radcliffe,' said Julie. 'He's one of our consultants and an authority on dementia. He's written a couple of books on the subject.'

'Maybe we can see him tomorrow morning then. We're down there for the post-mortem. I'll ring him.'

'Be warned, he's a bit full of himself.'

'Harris will love that,' said Gallagher.

'You be home for tea?' she said. 'I should be getting off about four.'

'Hopefully but it feels like it won't be much before seven.'

'I'll see you when I see you then.'

The sergeant slipped the phone back into his pocket and noticed that the minivan and the ambulance were already rumbling down the track towards the main road. Guthrie was in the passenger seat of the Land Rover, leaving the sergeant standing alone outside the cottage. He felt a sudden chill, climbed into the driver's seat and started the engine.

'Definitely time to go,' he said.

'Too right,' said Guthrie.

Gallagher started the engine and began to edge the vehicle down the track, resisting the urge to look back.

# Chapter six

'So, I'm taking referrals from nurses now, am I?' said Neal Radcliffe. The psychiatrist shot a sly look across his desk at Gallagher. 'I'm honoured, I truly am.'

The sergeant resisted the urge to fire back a retort and instead left Harris to respond to the consultant's comment.

'Nurse Gallagher was only trying to be helpful when she recommended you,' said the inspector.

'I know,' said Radcliffe. 'I'm just pulling your leg. Sorry.'

It was shortly before 10:00am the next morning and Harris had travelled down the valley to the general hospital in Roxham where he had met up with Gallagher, who lived in the town. Now, the two detectives were sitting in the professor's spartan office on the third floor. Lying on a desk that was otherwise clear was a print-out of the scanned letter found in Hillview Cottage, which had been emailed to the psychiatrist late the previous afternoon.

'So, I've read the letter,' said Radcliffe. 'What do you want to know?'

'Do you think it's written by someone with dementia or not?' asked Harris.

'What makes you think that it isn't?'

'A lot of what it says does not add up. Then there's all this stuff about thinking he's the last man alive. Not to go outside these four walls, Professor, but whoever wrote it was clever enough to weave a web of false identities so the letter could easily be a fabrication designed to confuse us.'

'It could be,' said Radcliffe. 'However, it's not something to which I would like to commit myself. Not without meeting the patient in person, anyway. It's difficult to come to a prognosis from a single letter.'

'But we were told you are an authority on dementia,' said Gallagher.

'Your wife said that, did she?' said Radcliffe. He gave another sly smile. 'I'm flattered that a fellow professional holds me in such high regard. It means a lot.'

This time, Gallagher could not contain himself.

'Look,' he said, getting to his feet, 'if you don't want to help us, we can just as easily…'

Harris placed a restraining hand on the sergeant's shoulder. Gallagher hesitated for a few moments then nodded and sat down.

'I'm sorry,' he said.

'Just me having a little fun with your colleague,' said Radcliffe. He looked at Harris, assuming that the inspector would go along with the joke.

'Well, can I suggest that you don't,' said the inspector. 'Matthew's father died of dementia. Besides, he's right, we were told that you were an expert but if you're just out to waste our time, we'll go and find someone useful.'

'No need for that,' said Radcliffe hurriedly. 'It's just that I have to be careful. I have a reputation to protect.'

'Right,' said Harris. He didn't do reputations.

'What you have to realise, though, is that dementia is a highly complex area of study and that it is impossible to make snap judgements. Even people with my level of expertise find it challenging.'

'Can you not at least give us *something*?' said Harris. 'We really do need to know if we're dealing with someone who has genuinely lost his mind.'

'I could certainly give it some thought. Maybe show it to some colleagues working in the field, see what they think. But it could be several days, they're very busy people and–'

'We need to know now.'

'Why the urgency?'

Harris hesitated; he had deliberately not mentioned the previous day's events because he wanted to keep the investigation low profile until he had a better sense of what he was dealing with. He decided that the time had come to take the professor into his confidence.

'It's urgent,' he said, pointing to the letter, 'because whoever wrote that is part of a murder case.'

'Murder? You didn't mention anything about murder. There's been nothing on the news.'

'The media don't know about it yet,' said Harris.

'Is the man who wrote the letter a suspect or the victim?'

'We don't know but we can't rule out that he may be a suspect so anything you can tell us about him, however speculative, would be appreciated.'

Radcliffe picked up the note from the desk and studied it again.

'Well,' he said after a couple of minutes, 'it's written with a sense of structure that you would not normally associate with a confused mind. Having said that, people with dementia are perfectly capable of undergoing spells of clarity and displaying ordered thought. Treating dementia can be a very inexact science, as I am sure your sergeant here knows if his father suffered from it.'

'This stuff about thinking he's the last person alive,' said Harris. 'Does that ring true?'

'People with dementia can be susceptible to all sorts of imaginings, Chief Inspector. They can come over as perfectly rational then suddenly let slip that they think they're Napoleon.' Radcliffe's confidence was returning and he gave the detectives another sly look. 'I don't suppose you found a bicorne in the cottage, did you?'

The officers looked bewildered and Radcliffe chuckled.

'I'm sorry,' he said. 'A little psychiatry joke. Sometimes, I find it difficult to resist the chance to inject a little levity into proceedings. Napoleon wore a hat called a bicorne.'

The detectives said nothing.

'However,' said Radcliffe hurriedly, 'thinking that you are the last person alive is not a delusion that I have encountered in my thirty years in the job. It could be genuine or part of an act. I'd really need to sit down with the author to be certain.'

'Well, thank you for your help anyway,' said Harris. He stood up. 'One last question, do you think he could be dangerous?'

'There we enter into the realms of speculation.' The professor held out the letter. 'Would you like this back?'

'No, you keep it. Maybe you could let some of your colleagues take a look, like you suggested.'

'I'll see what I can do.' The consultant watched as the detectives headed for the door. 'Regards to your wife, Sergeant.'

'I just hope your road tax is up to date,' said Gallagher.

'Road tax?'

'Just a little police joke,' said Gallagher.

He stalked from the room and, once the detectives were out of the professor's earshot and walking down the corridor, the sergeant gave his boss an apologetic look.

'Sorry about losing it in there, guv,' he said. 'But the man's an arrogant twat. He reminds me of the consultant who dealt with my dad. I could have decked him for the insensitive way he told Dad that he was ill.'

'Sounds like the two of you were close.'

'We were. I'd have done anything for that man.'

'You were lucky,' said Harris. 'I had a terrible relationship with my father. He couldn't handle it when I kept getting into trouble when I was a teenager. He hated it when police came to the house and he was delighted when I left to join the Army. Said it would straighten me out. At least he was right about that.'

'Did you patch things up later then?' asked Gallagher.

'Not really. I only came back twice in my early years away but there wasn't any warmth between us. I only came back for my mother really. My father died not long after my second visit. I went to the funeral but, if I'm honest, I didn't feel anything.'

Gallagher shook his head vigorously.

'It was nothing like that with me and my father,' he said. 'I cried bucketloads when he died.'

'Are you sure you're OK to stick with this, because if it's painful for–'

Gallagher stopped walking.

'Thank you but I'll be fine,' he said. 'I won't deny that it has brought back a lot of painful memories, though. Dad was only sixty-three when he died and it was a terrible thing to watch him lose his mind. The thought of our guy wandering the hills in that kind of state does not bear thinking about.'

Harris reached out a hand and touched him lightly on the shoulder. Harris rarely engaged in physical contact and Gallagher felt tears welling up.

'Come on,' said Harris. 'Let's go and see Doc. Maybe a post-mortem will cheer you up.'

Gallagher chuckled.

'Maybe it will at that,' he said. 'And you get a cup of tea with Doc.'

# Chapter seven

Gillian Roberts was sitting at her desk at Levton Bridge Police Station, waiting for the arrival of a force press officer to discuss the news release on the murder, when there was a knock on the office door. Alison Butterfield walked into the room and the detective inspector noted the excited look on the young constable's face.

'You look like someone with news to impart,' said Roberts.

'We may have a name for our guy in the tent. Forensics managed to decipher some of the chassis number on the car.' The constable handed over a computer print-out. 'The DVLA has narrowed it down to half a dozen vehicles. The last one on the list is the one that interests us most, I would suggest.'

Roberts scanned the list.

'David Stabler,' she said thoughtfully. 'Now that name sounds familiar.'

'He's just been reported missing by his mother. Sally's running some checks on him at the moment. How come you know him, ma'am?'

'Not sure but there's something nagging away at the back of my mind.' Roberts thought for a few moments then shook her head. 'Nope, it won't come, but I've definitely read the name somewhere.'

There was a knock on the door and Sally Orr entered. The detective constable's eyes gleamed with excitement.

'Someone else with news, I sense,' said Roberts. 'You two in competition with each other?'

Orr placed another computer print-out on the desk.

'This came up when I googled the name David Stabler,' she said. 'It's the home page from his website. He's a journalist.'

Roberts scanned the print-out and clicked her fingers.

'Of course, he is,' she said. 'I knew I recognised the name.'

Before she could elaborate, a woman in her fifties walked into the room.

'Hope I'm not disturbing anything,' said Gina Jeffers, the force's senior press officer. She noticed the print-out lying on the desk. 'Ah, our David. How come you are interested in him then?'

'We think he may be our body at Haggs Scarr,' said Roberts.

'Really?' exclaimed the press officer. She gave a low whistle. 'Well, that will open a can of worms, if it's true.'

'It will?'

'It certainly will,' said Jeffers. 'He's walked a fine line for years. If it *is* him, it makes your investigation a whole lot more complicated. There's plenty of folks with reason to dislike him…'

* * *

Harris and Gallagher finished their mugs of tea and followed the white-haired Home Office pathologist out of his office and into the examination room, switching off their mobile phones as they did so at his request. For the next half an hour, they watched in silence as Doc probed the remains of the body found in the tent. When he had finished, having extracted a bullet from the mangled skull and dropped it into a metal bowl, the pathologist gave a grunt of satisfaction and straightened up.

'No surprises, I am guessing?' said Harris.

'It certainly doesn't take a genius to work out that death would have been pretty much instantaneous,' said Doc. 'He was shot with some sort of handgun at very close range. The angle the bullet went in would suggest that it might have happened during a struggle.'

'Accidental?' asked Gallagher.

'Possibly but I'd still go for murder.'

'When did it happen?' asked the sergeant.

'A couple of days ago. Difficult to be more precise what with the weather up there over the past two days. I'll give the bullet to Ballistics. See if they can match it to anything else.'

'Anything to help with identifying him?' asked Harris.

'Nothing to speak of. His fingerprints are not on record so it's safe to assume he's not got a criminal record. I'll check DNA and dental records and I'll ring you if I turn anything up. It could take a while, mind. There's not a lot to go on. No, for the moment you've got yourself a John Doe.'

The detectives nodded their appreciation.

'You've restored my faith in the medical profession after meeting Neal Radcliffe,' said Gallagher.

'Not difficult,' said Doc. 'The man's an arse.'

Chuckling at the comment, the detectives walked out into the corridor and turned on their mobile phones. The inspector's device was the first to issue a ping denoting a message, followed seconds later by Gallagher's. Harris listened to his message and rang Roberts.

'Sorry,' he said. 'We were in the PM. You've got a name for our dead guy then?'

'Looks like it. And he's someone who may well have plenty of enemies in the world of organised crime.'

'Are you sure about that?' asked Harris. 'According to Doc, he's not coming up on any of our databases.'

'I'm sure,' said Roberts. 'In fact, you can read all about it.'

# Chapter eight

That afternoon, Jack Harris stood in the briefing room in Levton Bridge Police Station and surveyed the assembled detectives. There was a sense of excitement among the officers as they waited for him to begin talking. The fact that the murdered man appeared to be a journalist had given the inquiry an additional frisson of intrigue, not to mention numerous potential lines of inquiry. Behind Harris on the wall was a noticeboard upon which would normally have been pinned photographs of persons of interest. However, this time there was only the print-out from David Stabler's website. No photographs of anyone. It looked very bare.

'For the moment, we are assuming that the dead man is David Stabler,' said Harris. He turned to tap the print-out. 'This is here because we have been unable to track down a picture. However, Gina is going to tell you what we know about him.

The press officer walked to the front of the room.

'David Stabler may have been camera-shy,' she said, 'but he was known to just about every police press officer in the land, which is ironic because he didn't have much time for any of us. He specialised in organised crime and obtained his information from contacts from within police forces and the criminal fraternity. He was remarkably well-connected.'

'Who did he work for?' asked Gallagher.

'He worked as a crime reporter for a couple of the national tabloids in London for the best part of a decade until he was in his early thirties, then went freelance ten years ago. He still supplied the nationals with stories.'

'What kind of stories?' asked Butterfield.

'Sensationalist crime stuff, mainly,' said Jeffers. 'Do you remember the front-page story that *The Daily News* ran a few weeks ago? The one revealing that a detective superintendent in the Met had been suspended for starting a relationship with a gang leader's wife?'

There were blank faces except for Gallagher's.

'Midas,' he said. He noticed the perplexed expressions on the faces of the other detectives. 'He's a big London villain. Real name Francis Jacques, but known as Midas because everything he touches turns to gold. He lives up to it, too – big house, gold bath taps and the like. The story in *The Daily News* didn't name him but everyone knew it was his missus. It was down to David Stabler, was it, Gina?'

'It was. A pal of mine in the Met Press Office reckons that he got the story from one of his contacts within the force. Someone in CID. Apparently, it caused quite a stir.'

'Sure did,' said Gallagher. 'I was talking to one of my mates in the Met and he said that the top brass were running round like headless chickens trying to find out who leaked the information to him. There were memos flying everywhere.'

'Don't get the wrong idea about Stabler, though,' said Jeffers. 'He was not just a foot-in-the-door merchant. He did the sensationalist stuff because it brought in the good money but he also wrote more considered pieces. They paid less but were much more his thing. They usually appeared in a magazine called *The Organisation*. It's popular with academics and criminology students.'

'And police officers,' said Roberts. 'That's where I recognised his name from. It's a decent read. Really in-depth stuff. You said he didn't like police press officers, Gina? How come? Surely, you are there to help people like him?'

'Not if you listened to what David Stabler said about us,' replied Jeffers. 'In his opinion, we are only there to stop good stories getting out. He reckoned that he could get the information without our help and there were certainly plenty of officers who talked to him. David tended to come to press officers only when he wanted a comment on a story, and usually at the last minute so we had no time to prevent publication. That's what happened with the Midas story. *The Daily News* rang up half an hour before their deadline.'

'Had he contacted us for anything in our area?' asked Gallagher.

'He had, yes.' Jeffers glanced at Harris. 'He wanted to write a profile on Jack for *The Organisation*.'

All eyes turned to the inspector.

'He'd been trying for years,' said Harris. 'He started asking when I was running the Greater Manchester Police gangs initiative. I didn't fancy being interviewed and the Press Office kept saying no but he kept pestering them. He was persistent, I'll give him that.'

'Did you ever meet him?' asked Roberts.

'Only the once. He approached me outside a police station in Manchester and demanded to know why I wouldn't talk to him. He was hiding in the shadows in the car park.' Harris gave a slight smile at the memory. 'Not the greatest of tactics when you are approaching an officer who has just heard that a gang leader has put a price on his head. I sent him away with a flea in his ear.'

'He's lucky that he's got an ear left,' said Gallagher.

A ripple of laughter ran round the room.

'Stabler tried a couple more times when I moved up here,' said Harris when the laughter had died away. 'But we hadn't heard from him for the best part of a year. We reckoned that he must have given up, didn't we, Gina?'

'Not sure David Stabler did "giving up",' said Jeffers.

'So, are we saying that he was up here because he was investigating a story?' asked Butterfield.

'It's certainly possible,' said Harris. 'Gina, you heard anything on the grapevine?'

'Nothing. Not that that means anything – like I said, police press officers were usually the last ones to hear when it came to David Stabler.'

'It's not beyond the bounds of possibility that he could have been shot because of the Midas story,' said Gallagher. 'According to my mate, Midas was furious when it came out. Ranting and raving, saying that the article had made him a laughing stock – and you don't do that if you want to stay healthy.'

'We certainly should not discount anything at this stage,' said Harris. 'And we should not forget the reference in the letter found at Hillview Cottage to a wildlife photographer camping exactly where we found the body, or the fact that the German police are interested in our missing guy.'

'Which would seem to make him our prime suspect,' said Roberts. 'And suggest that the dementia stuff *is* as we suspected, something designed to confuse us.'

'Which is why we have to find out who he is,' said Harris. 'Alison, I want you and Sally to keep digging around for anything on him. I take it we've had no more sightings of him?'

'We've asked just about everyone we can think of, but no one saw him,' said Butterfield. 'It's like he vanished into thin air after the murder.'

Harris gave her a sharp look.

'I said I didn't want to hear talk like that,' he said. 'There is always a rational explanation for these things. He's as real as they come and I don't like the idea of him running round with a gun in his hand. We would all do well to remember that.'

'Sorry, sir,' said Butterfield. She flushed red and looked down at her shoes.

Harris glanced at the young plainclothes officer sitting next to her.

'Alistair,' he said, 'I want you to come up with a list of recent articles written by Stabler. Let's see if we can't find anyone else with a motive to kill him.'

'I'll get right on it,' said Detective Constable Alistair Marshall. He glanced at Jeffers. 'Gina, I could do with a helping hand.'

She nodded.

'But first of all, we have to confirm that the body is definitely David Stabler,' said Harris. 'He was reported missing by his mother. Gillian, can you get in touch with her?'

'Already on it,' said Roberts. 'What will you be doing?'

'I think a trip to Manchester may be in order,' said Harris. 'I seem to recall that *The Organisation* is published by a small company in the city.'

'In the meantime,' said Jeffers, 'do we need to issue a press release about the body? We've had a call from a local radio journalist who said she'd heard that the police helicopter was out at Haggs Scarr yesterday. I can't keep stalling her for ever.'

'Just so long as we don't name Stabler,' said Harris. He gave everyone a stern look. 'And I want this kept as low profile as possible for the moment. The last thing we want is journalists getting in the way. I want us to control the agenda on this one.'

'An approach of which I'm sure David Stabler would have heartily disapproved,' said Jeffers.

With the briefing concluded, the inspector returned to his office, where he topped up the dogs' water bowl, gave the animals some treats, sat down at his desk and made a call on his mobile.

'Now then, matey,' said a man's voice. 'What do you want us to solve for you this time?'

'Cheeky git,' said Harris. He tipped back on his chair and put his feet up on the desk. 'But I *am* after some help, Graham.'

'Getaway,' said Leckie. A uniformed constable with Greater Manchester Police, he was one of the inspector's few close friends, the men having met when Harris worked in the city. Even though Harris had returned home to Levton Bridge, they still talked on a regular basis because Leckie worked in Greater Manchester's force intelligence unit and a number of the area's thieves committed crimes in the valley. 'What are you after then?'

'I've got a dead body on my hands,' said Harris. 'We think that it might be a journalist called David Stabler. Shot in the face.'

'Well, there was always the possibility that it might happen one day. From what I hear, he took plenty of risks, did our Mr Stabler. What do you need from me?'

'I'm looking to come down to Manchester to see the publisher of *The Organisation* magazine. Bloke called Chris Steward. Wondered if you know if he's trustworthy or the type to run straight to the national newspapers with the story?'

'I only know him by reputation. Never met him. He's a former journalist on one of the broadsheets. *The Telegraph*, I think. He's sound enough, from what I hear, but then I would never trust any journalist when there's a good story afoot.'

'We're just going to have to risk it, I guess,' said Harris. 'I don't suppose you've heard if Stabler was working on anything that would get him killed, have you?'

'Sorry, old son, my contract says that if I deal with journalists, I'm out doing school crossing patrols until I retire. I'll ask a few questions on the QT, though.'

'While I'm on, you wouldn't happen to know anything about any German criminals operating in the UK, would you?'

'There's the odd one kicking about,' said Leckie. 'Why so interested?'

'Because I've also got a missing John Doe who might be involved with German criminals. A retired guy.'

'What's he done? Defrauded the Post Office on his television licence?'

'It might be a little heavier than that.'

'I can ask around, if you like.'

'Just so long as I can trust you to keep it discreet,' said Harris. 'It's a sensitive one.'

'I'm an intelligence officer. Of course, you can't trust me.'

'I'm serious, Graham.'

'Surely, you know me well enough to know I'll play it right,' said Leckie. He sounded offended. 'When have I ever let you down?'

'I'm sorry,' said Harris. 'I've got Special Branch on my back and they've turned me paranoid.'

'Well, why didn't you say? Special Branch are enough to turn anyone paranoid. Give me a ring when you have more info.'

'Will do,' said Harris.

# Chapter nine

Gillian Roberts gestured for her visitor to take a seat and walked over to the kettle in the corner of her office. As she did so, the detective inspector shot David Stabler's mother a surreptitious look. Something about Margie Stabler had unsettled the detective from the moment that she had arrived at Levton Bridge Police Station, a sense that she was somehow detached from events, as if she did not fully understand what was happening to her. The detective attributed it to grief.

'Would you like a cup of tea?' asked the inspector.

Margie nodded but did not speak. It was 10:00am and a patrol car from West Yorkshire Police had brought her up to Levton Bridge from her home in Leeds. Roberts flicked the switch on the kettle and continued to study her visitor. Margie did not make for an encouraging sight for a few more moments. Roberts estimated that she was in her mid-fifties but her unkempt appearance made her look older. Her straggly dark hair was streaked with grey and looked like it had not been combed for several days and her green woollen jumper was threadbare with a hole in one elbow. The overall impression was one of neglect. Roberts suspected that the same could be said of Margie's relationship with her son. The detective inspector was beginning to understand the reason for David Stabler's independent approach to life.

'I'm sorry I did not recognise any of David's belongings,' said Margie. It was as if she could sense what the detective inspector was thinking.

'No reason why you should,' said Roberts. She handed Margie a steaming mug of tea and sat down behind her desk. 'I'm not sure that I would recognise any of my boys' camping gear.'

'How old are they?' asked Margie as she took a sip of tea.

'Teenagers. One at secondary school, one at college.'

'And are you close to them?'

'I like to think so.'

'I wasn't close to David,' said Margie sadly. 'Not even when he was young. He was a very secretive child, and it got worse after his father left. I only found out that David had fallen in with a bad lot when one of the other mothers told me.'

'What kind of a bad lot? We're trying to build up a picture of his life and anything you can tell us will be helpful.'

'Drugs,' said Margie. 'Cannabis to start with, then amphetamines. He received a couple of warnings from the police. They said he could end up being sent to a juvenile centre if he did not stop.'

'And did he?'

'I don't know. We drifted even further apart after that.' Margie gave her a helpless look. 'To be honest, I don't know how much I can help you. I don't really know much about David's life. I suppose you think that makes me a bad mother?'

Roberts thought back to an incident a couple of years previously when she only discovered that one of her sons had taken drugs at a party weeks after it happened, and even then, it had been only when one of his friends accidentally let the information slip out. The detective inspector remembered how devastated she had felt, as if a bond with her son had been severed. Like Margie, she had been overwhelmed by a sense that she had failed in her duty as a mother. Realising that Margie was expecting a reply, Roberts shook her head.

'No, it doesn't make you a bad mother,' she said. 'Teenagers do tend to go their own way.'

'David certainly did. He did not seem to care what effect he was having on anyone but himself.'

Margie gave another helpless look and there was a heavy silence in the room for a few moments then she looked at the detective inspector with eyes that glistened with tears.

'Are you sure that it's him?' she asked.

'It's a strong possibility.'

'And are you sure that I can't view the body?'

'I don't think that would be a good idea. It's not very… he was shot in the face… I'm sure you can imagine.'

Margie stifled a sob. Roberts gave her time to regain her composure.

'When did you last talk to your son?' asked the detective.

'Six months ago.'

'That long?' Roberts cursed herself inwardly for letting the surprise show.

'I know what you must think of me but I did try to keep in touch with David, really I did, but he was always changing his mobile phone number. I had to wait for him to ring me.' Margie gave a mirthless laugh. 'I didn't even know his address. Can you believe that? A mother who doesn't even know where her son lives?'

'We are working on the theory that he may have angered somebody with something that he wrote.'

Margie gave the detective inspector a bewildered look.

'I had no idea he was in danger,' she said. 'This has all come as a terrible shock.'

Roberts was silent for a few moments, marvelling at how little David Stabler's mother knew about her son's life. The detective inspector may have worried constantly about her relationship with her teenage boys but she was pretty certain that she would know if they were in danger. That they would tell her, come to their mother for help. The detective frowned – or would they? If she was brutally honest with herself, she could not be sure.

'Did he ever give the impression that he was worried about anything?' asked Roberts.

'He always accused me of meddling if I asked about his work. I know that if it ever got too stressful, he would take himself off camping. He'd always loved the hills. Sometimes, he'd be away for weeks.'

'So, how come you reported him missing this time?' asked Roberts.

'Because he did not ring on my birthday on Sunday. We might not have talked much but David never missed my birthday. When he failed to get in touch, I knew that something had happened to him.'

Tears started in Margie's eyes again.

'But I never thought that it would be anything like this,' she said. 'I mean, who would ever think of murdering my David?'

# Chapter ten

'I can't say I am surprised that David Stabler has been murdered,' said Chris Steward. The publisher of *The Organisation* turned round from making the tea to look at Harris and Gallagher. 'I don't think anyone who knew him would be surprised, either.'

'Why's that?' asked Harris.

It was 10:00am and the detectives were sitting on the fourth floor of a non-descript office block in Manchester in a room whose walls were lined with books and magazines. Steward, a bespectacled man in his mid-thirties, handed them their tea and sat down, taking a few moments to find a space for his own mug among the mass of newspaper cuttings and computer print-outs sprawled across his desk.

'Did you ever meet him?' he asked.

'Once,' said Harris. 'He wanted to interview me for your magazine. He was very persistent.'

'That was David, alright. What you have to realise is that he was not like most journalists. Too many of them these days rely on press releases and social media but not David. He believed in getting under the skin of a story and he was obsessive about it. Some might even say that he was reckless.'

'Reckless enough to get himself killed?' asked Gallagher.

'All I can say is that all he was interested in was the story and I don't think he minded how he got it. There was this wild look in his eyes when he talked about his work, like he was challenging you to disagree with the way he was going about things. He'd had numerous threats down the years, but it didn't stop him.'

'What kind of threats?' asked Harris.

'Death threats. We've taken some of the calls here. Criminals don't like seeing their darkest secrets plastered all over the newspapers.'

'Who were the calls from?'

'Anonymous but you can work it out. There was one last year after he'd written a piece on the Triads and we've had a couple this year, one in January after we published a piece about people smuggling and most recently after he wrote something about Moroccan criminals trying to muscle in on the London drugs scene for our latest edition.'

Steward reached backwards, took a copy of his magazine down from a shelf and passed it over to the sergeant.

'Starts on page 42,' he said. 'As it turns out, it could be his epitaph. Oh, and he'd been attacked as well.'

'When?' asked Gallagher.

'Two or three months ago. He was renting a place in Wakefield and a couple of guys jumped him in the street and tried to grab his bag with his laptop in it. He said he'd never run so fast in his life. Coughed his guts up – he'd always been a heavy smoker.'

'Did he describe his attackers?' asked Gallagher.

'Just that they both had shaved heads. Oh, and one of them had bad breath. David described him as weasel-faced. He left town after that.'

'Did you not try to warn him that he was putting his life at risk?'

'He wouldn't have listened to me,' said Steward. 'He wouldn't have listened to anyone. Like I say, David Stabler was unlike most other journalists I have known. Anything to get the story. A dying breed.'

'And now he's a dead one,' said Harris.

'Indeed.'

'Who were these guys who attacked him?'

'If he knew, he didn't say,' said Steward. 'Not that he would, anyway. Having said that, your visit is not exactly a surprise. He was due to ring me for one of our regular chats about feature ideas and it wasn't like him to miss. He'd changed his mobile number so I couldn't get hold of him. He did that a lot, did David. You had to wait for him to ring you.'

'Did he ever mention a criminal called Francis Jacques?' asked Harris. 'He's based in London.'

'Oh, I know all about Midas, Chief Inspector. Everyone knows about Midas. The only thing David said was that he thought there would be hell on earth when the story about Midas's wife appeared in the paper.' Steward surveyed the detectives keenly. 'Do you think Midas could have something to do with David's death? He was livid when the story was published and he tried every which way to find out who had given David the information.'

'And who had?' asked Gallagher.

'A good journalist never divulges his contacts, Sergeant.'

'Not even a dead one? I mean, there is nothing to stop you…'

'Even if I knew where he got his information from, you'd not find me handing details of his contacts over to you,' said Steward. 'I have to consider their safety as well but, for what it's worth, I can't see Midas killing David over something like that. He knows that murdering a journalist ups the ante big time.'

'Was David working on anything else that might have led these two men to come after him?' asked Harris.

Steward hesitated; it was the first time during the conversation that his demeanour had lost some of its assurance. It was only the slightest of hesitation but it was enough for Jack Harris.

'I think you know more that you're letting on,' said Harris. He fixed the publisher with a stare. 'And I'm perfectly prepared to conduct this conversation on a more official footing if you try to keep things from us.'

'David swore me to secrecy.' Steward held up his hands as Harris opened his mouth to reply. 'OK, OK, I know, now that he's dead... look, all I know is that he was working on a book. He wouldn't tell me what it was about, just that it would be big news when it came out. There's been plenty of speculation about its contents among the criminal fraternity.'

'Do you think he wanted you to publish it?' asked Gallagher.

'He never said that he did.'

'So, he had another publisher lined up then?'

'Possibly. I don't know.' Steward noticed their sceptical expressions. 'Honestly, I don't. David said the fewer people knew about it the better and he was not the kind of man you pushed.'

Ten minutes later, the detectives stood up and prepared to leave the office, armed with Stabler's last known address in Sheffield, gleaned from his most recent invoice sent to the magazine.

'One thing before you go, Chief Inspector,' said Steward. He opened the door for them. 'How come you never let David interview you? I can see a really striking front cover with you and your dogs on the hills.'

'It's not my style. And don't you ask me, either, because the answer's the same. And I'd appreciate it if you'd keep what we have talked about to yourself.'

'You can trust me,' said Steward.

Once the detectives were back in the street, Gallagher looked at Harris.

'Great,' he said. 'A murder with a whole criminal underworld as our suspects. And there was us thinking that it would turn out to be complicated!'

'Indeed,' said Harris. He looked up at the office window and saw Steward watching the detectives as they headed for the Land Rover. He was talking into his mobile phone. 'What do you make of him?'

'I've not yet come across a journalist I trust,' said Gallagher.

The inspector nodded, took his mobile phone out of his pocket and rang Gillian Roberts. The detective inspector took the call as she stood at the top of the steps in front of Levton Bridge Police Station and watched Margie Stabler climb into the back of the police patrol car that was to take her back to Leeds.

'How'd it go with Steward?' she asked.

'We've turned up three thousand suspects,' said Harris.

'At least you've narrowed it down.'

'How'd it go with Mum?' asked Harris. 'She got anything?'

Roberts watched as the patrol car started off up the hill towards the marketplace with a pale-faced Margie Stabler staring out of the rear window.

'Just regrets,' she said.

## Chapter eleven

It was just after 1:00pm when Harris guided the Land Rover into the Victorian terraced street on the fringes of Sheffield city centre. Gallagher glanced down at the invoice on his lap and pointed to a rundown house with grimy windows and flaking paint.

'That's it,' he said. 'Number eleven. Salubrious, eh?'

Harris parked the vehicle and the officers walked up the weed-infested path. As they did so, the front door was opened by a thin-faced man in tattered jeans and a threadbare jumper. He eyed them suspiciously.

'You from the council?' he asked. 'Because I've had enough of you people trying to–'

'I'm Chief Inspector Harris.' The DCI flashed his warrant card. 'This is Detective Sergeant Gallagher. And you are?'

'Geoff Riley. I'm the landlord.'

'Well, Mr Riley, we're looking for David Stabler.'

'Aren't we all?' said the landlord. 'I haven't seen him for weeks.'

'Can we see his flat?'

'Why would you want to do that?'

'I'd rather not say,' said Harris. 'But I can make this official, if you want. Get a warrant.'

Riley shook his head and stood aside to allow them to enter the dingy hallway with its faded carpet and a musty smell that had them wrinkling their noses.

'How long had David been renting the room from you?' asked Harris.

'A couple of months. It was only a short-term lease. He was due to leave at the end of the month. Look, what is this about?'

'We think he may be dead.'

'That's a pity,' said Riley. 'He owed me for his final two weeks. I don't suppose you can give me the address of a relative so I can bill them, can you?'

Gallagher looked at Harris and raised an eyebrow. People, thought the sergeant sadly, they never failed to amaze him. Riley noticed the gesture.

'Business is business,' he said defensively. 'A man's got to eat.'

'Right,' said Gallagher.

'When did you last see David?' asked Harris as Riley led them up the gloomy stairs.

'Three, four weeks ago.'

'How did he seem?'

'We didn't speak – and he hasn't been back since, as far as I know.'

'Did you not think that was odd?' asked Gallagher as they reached the first floor landing. 'Renting a room and not staying in it?'

Riley shrugged.

'People come and go in places like this,' he said. 'You learn not to ask questions. I only take notice when they fall behind with their rent.'

He unlocked a door.

'This is his,' he said.

The officers entered the room, which was sparsely furnished and had little in the way of personal belongings.

The walls were bare apart from an out-of-date calendar hanging in a corner.

'I was going to wait until the two weeks were up then let it to someone else,' said Riley. 'I imagine that I can do that now, can I?'

'Not until we've checked it,' said Harris. 'And confirmed that he's dead.'

'But I need to get someone in so that I–'

'You really are full of the milk of human kindness, aren't you?' said Gallagher. He gave the landlord a disgusted look. 'Anyway, can you leave us alone for a few minutes, please? We need to search the room.'

Riley looked as if he was going to remonstrate but thought better of it and left, muttering under his breath.

'You come across such a delightful breed of scumbags in this job, don't you?' said Gallagher.

Harris nodded and the detectives listened to Riley's shoes clattering on the stair floorboards. When the sound had receded, the inspector looked round the room.

'Not that searching it will take long,' he said.

'Reminds me of Hillview Cottage,' said Gallagher. 'Impersonal. Nothing of the man.'

Harris opened the wardrobe to reveal several shirts and a couple of pairs of trousers on hangers. Gallagher looked in the chest of drawers but all he found was a couple of old T-shirts. He moved onto the bedside table drawers but they were all empty. The remainder of the search only took a few minutes and after it was completed, Harris sat on the bed, looked at the walls and shook his head.

'Say hello to Mr Nobody,' he said.

'Indeed,' said Gallagher. He walked over to the ramshackle table in the window on which sat a mug, the ring round the edge suggesting that it had once contained tea. 'And where's his laptop? He must have had one if he was writing a book but it's not here and we didn't find it at the campsite.'

'Whoever killed him must have it. We need to know what that book's about, Matty lad.'

Gallagher glanced down into the street where Riley finished a cigarette, ground the stub into the pavement and looked up at him before heading back up the path. The sergeant turned back into the room.

'Mr Charming is on his way back,' he said. 'What do you want do? You want to get Forensics in?'

'Possibly but I'm not sure what good it will do us. Stabler was killed at Haggs Scarr and there's no sign of anything having happened here.'

'So, you're going to allow chummy to let the place out again? Please tell me you aren't. I'd love to see the look on his face.'

'Not sure I can justify hanging onto it much longer,' said Harris.

Riley appeared at the door.

'You finished?' he asked.

'Just about,' said Harris. He stood up. 'What did you know about David Stabler, Mr Riley?'

'Like I said, you don't really get to know people in this business. They don't tend to stay long.'

Gallagher looked round the room.

'I wonder why not?' he said.

Riley gave him a dirty look but said nothing.

'Did he ever have any visitors?' asked Harris. 'A girlfriend, perhaps?'

'I never saw anyone,' said Riley. 'There was a couple of men came round asking questions about him but that was about it.'

The detectives gave him a sharp look.

'What kind of men?' asked Harris.

'Rough types. Young lads. Shaved heads. They wanted to know where he was.' Riley shuddered. 'I were glad that I didn't know. They looked really mean. One of them had really bad breath, I do remember that.'

'When was this?' asked the inspector.

'A couple of weeks back.'

'Did you let them into the room?'

'I weren't going to say no to fellas like that. They was only in a couple of minutes, though. Whatever they were looking for, they didn't find it.'

'Did they give any names?' asked Gallagher.

'Na,' said Riley. 'And I wasn't going to ask them neither. I was relieved when they headed off back to London, I can tell you.'

'London?' said Gallagher. 'Are you sure?'

'That's what their voices sounded like anyway.' Riley led them back out onto the landing. 'So, when can I have the room then?'

'Not for a while,' said Harris. 'Not now that we know about the men from London. Could be a while, eh, Sergeant?'

Gallagher grinned.

'I reckon so,' he said.

'But…' began Riley.

Harris turned on the stairs and gave the landlord a hard look.

'But nothing,' he said. 'No one gets into this room until I say so. Understand?'

Riley looked like he was about to continue his protestations but one look at the stern expression on Harris's face was enough to banish the idea once more. He nodded gloomily.

'I take it you'll also want the thing that I found in his room?' he said.

'What thing?' asked Harris.

'I dunno,' said Riley. 'It's some sort of legal document. Must have fallen out of his bag. I found it on the floor when I was checking if he'd gone. I wondered if it was what the men were after but they never asked about it, so I said nothing. Like I say, it doesn't pay to get involved in this business.'

'Show us,' said Harris.

At the bottom of the stairs, the detectives followed Riley towards the back of the house and into his cluttered little office, where the landlord unlocked a wall safe and withdrew a brown A4 envelope, which he handed to Harris. The seal had been broken and Riley noticed the looks on the detectives' faces.

'I never did that,' he said. 'I didn't. I have no idea what it is. I never looked at it.'

'And yet you knew that it was a legal document,' said Gallagher.

Riley looked uncomfortable but said nothing. The detectives left the house and emerged out of its stale stench into the blessed fresh air of the street, where they headed over to the Land Rover.

'What a sleaze-ball,' said Gallagher.

Harris unlocked the Land Rover, climbed into the driver's seat and slid the document from the envelope.

'What is it?' asked Gallagher after giving his boss time to scan the contents.

'Looks like he *did* have a publisher lined up for the book. In London, oddly enough.' Harris passed the document over to the sergeant. 'It's a contract. It doesn't give any more information about the book itself, but whatever it's about, they were prepared to pay him a healthy advance. I think that we can safely assume that it's what the men were looking for.'

'It's looking more and more likely that it's about Midas. All roads seem to be pointing to London.'

'They certainly are,' said Harris. He started the engine. 'How do you fancy popping down to Da Smoke tomorrow?'

Gallagher beamed.

'Always,' he said.

As Harris drove through the city, Gallagher spent his time arranging for a forensics officer to visit Stabler's room then left a message on the answerphone of the publisher in London. After completing the tasks, he made several attempts to re-initiate a conversation with the inspector but they all came to nothing and the detectives travelled in silence for a while, each alone with their own thoughts. Harris had just guided the vehicle onto the northbound motorway when his mobile rang in its cradle on the dashboard.

'Doc,' he said, taking the call. 'You got some news for me?'

'We've managed to track down an old dental record for David Stabler,' said the pathologist. 'He's your dead guy, alright. And Ballistics have been on about the bullet I dug out of the body. It's definitely a handgun but it doesn't link up to any known weapon. Certainly not one that's been used in a crime.'

'That's a pity,' said Harris. 'We're struggling here.'

'Sorry,' said Doc.

As the inspector ended the call, it was the turn of Gallagher's mobile to ring. He spoke for a couple of minutes then slipped his phone back into his jacket pocket.

'That was the chief executive's PA at Sudden Death Books,' he explained. 'We've got a meeting at their offices in Holborn at two o'clock tomorrow. I thought it best not to say why we want to see them. Not until we're down there, anyway.'

'Probably for the best,' said Harris. He pulled into the fast lane of the motorway to overtake a string of lorries. 'The less people know about the book the better. Did you get the impression that they were expecting the call?'

'The PA certainly didn't seem that surprised.'

'I'm not liking the way this one's playing out, Matty lad,' said Harris. 'I'm not comfortable with the idea of publishers and journalists being involved. I don't know who we can trust.'

'So, we do our usual then,' said Gallagher. 'Trust no one but ourselves.'

# Chapter twelve

Harris and Gallagher returned to Levton Bridge Police Station where the inspector picked up the dogs from the secretary who had been caring for them and took them for a walk through the fields surrounding the town. Occasionally, he cast wistful looks towards the hills, the summits of which were fast disappearing in the gathering late afternoon gloom. Jack Harris had always experienced an acute sense of resentment whenever his work took him away from his first love for too long. The hills were the reason he had returned to work in the valley and, without realising he had done it, he gave a heavy sigh. He was not looking forward to the following day's trip to London.

On his return to the police station, and with his mood little improved, he summoned Roberts and Gallagher to his office.

'Please tell me that someone has got some good news for me,' he said as they took their seats.

'I am afraid not,' said Gallagher. 'The Sheffield forensics guys checked out Stabler's bedsit for us but the prints don't match anyone with a record. Some are from the landlord but most match those taken from Stabler's body. Whoever the guys were who searched his room, they don't appear to have left any dabs.'

'Gloves?'

'Forensics reckon so, which would strengthen the idea that we are dealing with organised crime.'

'And what about our man at Hillview Cottage?' asked Harris. 'We anywhere nearer to identifying him?'

'We've got nowhere with the newspaper research yet,' said Roberts. 'It's like I feared. Some of the papers from that time have been moved onto digital but a lot of the stuff is still hardcopy or microfiche. It would help if we knew what we were looking for. We could be looking for something that is not actually there.'

'And where does he fit into the story anyway?' asked Gallagher. 'For all we know, the fact that Stabler was found near his cottage could be a coincidence. Maybe Bob Crowther is right and he'll turn up next year on the banks of a stream.'

'Maybe,' said Harris. He sighed. 'We're getting nowhere here.'

'There's still the book,' said Gallagher. His mobile phone rang and he looked at the name of the caller. 'Danny Mahler, my mate from the Met. He's a DC with one of the organised crime squads.'

The sergeant placed his phone on the desk.

'Danny, me old mucker,' he said. 'Thanks for ringing back. I've got my DCI and DI with me and you're on speaker. Any news?'

'I may have, yes. It looks like Midas knows that something has happened to David Stabler.'

'But our press release did not name him,' said Gallagher. 'Just said that an unidentified body had been found on the hills.'

'Well, he definitely knows that something has happened.'

'DCI Jack Harris here,' said the inspector. He leaned towards the phone. 'Do you think he knows because he had him killed, Danny?'

'He'd be a fool if he did. Midas is a shrewd operator and he knows that killing journalists brings a bucketload of shit down onto your head. It would seem that he is very interested in the book that Stabler was writing, though.'

'Is it about him then?' asked Harris.

'There's been some speculation among the criminals but no one seems to know for certain,' replied Mahler. 'However, I'd bet my pension that your guys in Sheffield were a couple of his heavies.'

'Why so sure?' asked Gallagher.

'Lee Garritt's got bad breath and he usually runs with a character called Max Rodney. Shaven head. Ex-heavyweight boxer. Nasty pieces of work, the both of them. They're Midas's main men and Midas can get pretty paranoid when he's got an idea in his head. Maybe we can meet up tomorrow after your meeting with the publisher? What time's your train back?'

'Just after seven.'

'Well, there's a nice little curry house not far from Euston Station if you fancy meeting up before you go,' said Mahler.

Gallagher glanced at Harris, who nodded his agreement.

'Sounds good,' said the sergeant. He ended the call. 'I would say that the picture just got a lot clearer, wouldn't you?'

'Except that we've picked up nothing about two shaven-headed Londoners coming into our area,' said Roberts. 'And given the way folks neb on each other round here, I'd have expected to hear something.'

Gallagher's smile faded.

'You're no fun, anymore,' he said.

# Chapter thirteen

Next morning, Harris and Gallagher caught the train to London, the inspector having again left his dogs in the care of one of the police station office staff. It was not something that he liked doing but the demands of the investigation had left him with no option. It was just past 1:00pm when the train entered the outskirts of the capital. Gallagher stared wistfully out of the window at the familiar factories, office developments, blocks of flats and terraced houses. A Londoner born and bred, he had always lived in the city until Julie had announced that she wanted to head back north to be near her parents. The suggestion had filled the sergeant with dread but he had reluctantly agreed to the move. Adapting to life in the North had been difficult but he had found himself slowly getting used to the change. Trips back to London always unsettled him, however, bringing with them pangs of regret at the life that he had left behind.

Jack Harris had no such thoughts. Sitting opposite his colleague, he stared out at the grey urban landscape with little enthusiasm. Although Harris had worked for the police in Manchester for a number of years after leaving the Army, he had never held any affection for big cities.

The inspector noted the look on Gallagher's face as he continued to stare out of the window.

'You still miss the old place, I guess,' said Harris.

'Always,' said Gallagher. 'It's home, after all. I take it that it does nothing for you?'

'Nothing at all,' said Harris. He gave a slight smile. 'Not enough sheep, I am afraid.'

Gallagher chuckled. He knew that glib comments about sheep uttered by urban police officers irritated Harris more than anything else.

'Do you know,' said the sergeant, 'I believe I'm getting somewhere in helping you develop a sense of humour.'

Five minutes later, the train pulled into Euston Station and the detectives headed out into the bustling city streets. Gallagher gave a happy sigh, relishing the noise and movement, while Harris wondered, as he always did when he visited cities, how anyone could enjoy living like this. They grabbed a quick lunch at a cafe near the station then hailed a taxi to take them to Holborn. Soon, they were sitting in the reception area of a concrete office block, waiting for the PA at Sudden Death Books to take them up to see the chief executive. A slim redhead in her twenties appeared after a few minutes.

'Sergeant Gallagher?' she asked.

'Guilty as charged,' said the detective. 'This is Detective Chief Inspector Harris.'

'Miranda Hayes,' she said. She extended a hand in welcome. 'I'm sorry to have kept you waiting but Miss Murrell is very busy. We have two book launches this week. However, she can spare you twenty minutes.'

'It might take longer than that,' said Harris.

'Well, like I say, she is very busy so I'd appreciate it if you could keep it as a brief as you can. I'll take you up.'

Harris scowled but said nothing and, after taking the lift to the third floor, the detectives were led into an office whose walls were lined with books. A smartly-dressed dark-haired woman in her thirties sat behind the desk.

Unlike the publisher of *The Organisation* the previous day, Heather Murrell's desk was clear. She stood up as the officers entered and extended an elegant hand, its fingernails polished and painted a luminescent green.

'Welcome to Sudden Death Books, gentlemen,' she said. 'Have you been offered a drink?'

'That would be welcome,' said Gallagher. 'Tea for both of us.'

Murrell nodded at her PA.

'Will you do the honours, please, Miranda?' she said. She held out her mug, which was decorated with the image of a bloodstained knife under the words "Sudden Death". 'And I'll have another chamomile, please.'

Miranda Hayes took the publisher's mug and left the room.

'So, how can I help you?' asked Murrell. Her demeanour was calm and courteous but not overly welcoming. She did not seem unsettled by the presence of two detectives in her office. 'It must be important to bring you all the way down here but my PA tells me that you were somewhat mysterious on the phone, Sergeant Gallagher.'

'It's a somewhat sensitive matter,' said Gallagher. 'We are investigating the murder of David Stabler. We heard that he was writing a book for you.'

'I assumed it was about that.' Murrell shook her head. 'A sad business.'

'You sound like you already knew that he was dead,' said Harris.

'I did, yes.'

'How come? We only put out the press release yesterday afternoon and we didn't name him.'

'News travels fast in my world, Chief Inspector.' Murrell gave a thin smile. 'And bad news travels fastest of all. I'm sure it's the same for you.'

'Did Chris Steward tell you?' asked Harris. He recalled the call that Steward made as the detectives left the office block the previous day.

'I'd rather not say. Do you think that the book might have something to do with David's death?'

'Possibly. And we are working on the theory that his killers might be from London.'

'Why would you think that?' asked Murrell.

'We have reason to believe that two men from London were tracking him. Have you heard of a man called Francis Jacques?'

'Everyone has heard of Midas,' said Murrell. 'But why would you want to know about him?'

'We wondered if the book was about him. We know David had written an article on his wife's affair. Maybe there was more to come. Is the book about Midas, Miss Murrell?'

'I am sure you can appreciate that such projects are bound up with a degree of confidentiality, Chief Inspector. The last thing we want is for any of those featured to ascertain the precise details so that they can take out injunctions to prevent its publication.'

'I think we can say with some confidence that we've gone way beyond injunctions,' said Harris. He produced a photocopy of the contract from his jacket pocket and placed it on the desk. 'We want to know what was so important about the book that you were prepared to pay David Stabler such a large advance – and why someone was prepared to resort to murder to stop him writing it.'

Consternation flickered across her face as she looked at the document.

'Where did you get this?' she demanded. 'I specifically told David that it was to be deposited with a lawyer.'

'He accidentally left it in his flat in Sheffield. It's possible that he had to leave in a hurry. He'd already been attacked once by the men who were trying to get the manuscript off him. Had he delivered it to you yet?'

'He hadn't, no,' said Murrell. 'He was well through the writing but said that he still had some final pieces of research to do – and it's pointless pushing me on the content, Chief Inspector. There's a non-disclosure agreement prohibiting anyone talking about the book. David had signed it.'

'Well, we haven't,' said Harris. 'And now that David is dead, he's unlikely to disclose much anyway, is he?'

'No, but the writer who has undertaken to complete the task has signed a similar agreement.'

The detectives looked at each other in alarm.

'Someone else is finishing the book?' said Harris. 'Who?'

'Suffice to say that he is a freelance based in the North of England. David was acutely aware of the risk he was running and had taken steps to ensure that the book was finished should anything happen to him.'

'And does this other author know that David is dead?' asked Harris.

'He does, yes.'

'Well, we'll need his name,' said Harris. There was urgency in his voice. 'He may well be in grave danger.'

Murrell hesitated.

'To use a literary allusion,' said Harris, 'to lose one author might be regarded as a misfortune but to lose two might be viewed as carelessness.'

Gallagher looked surprised; he could not recall ever hearing his boss use a literary allusion. Murrell thought for a few moments then nodded.

'His name's James Cronin,' she said. 'He lives in Leeds. He self-published a couple of real-life crime books after I turned them down, but he didn't sell many. I wasn't very happy when David told me what he'd done. I'd have rather handed the job over to one of our writers. I don't think James is up to it.'

'Why not?' asked Harris.

Murrell walked across the office and took a book down from a shelf. She handed it to Harris.

'That's one of them,' she said.

Harris looked at the lurid image of the smoking gun on the cover.

'*Inside Gangland*,' he said. 'What's wrong with that?'

'It's a cuttings job,' said Murrell dismissively. She returned to her seat. 'Taken from the newspapers. It's lazy journalism. I don't think James has the kind of contacts that David had, nor the tenacity, for that matter. Few journalists do.'

'Well, we'll need his contact details anyway,' said Harris as the PA entered the office bearing the tray of drinks. 'We need to get to him before someone else does.'

'I am sure that Miranda can let you have his phone number,' said Murrell. 'I don't know where he is, though. He said he was going to rent somewhere to finish the writing but he wouldn't tell me where. Did he mention anything to you, Miranda?'

'He didn't, no.' The PA handed over the mugs. 'And I'm not sure if he'll have his mobile switched on anyway. He said he was going to be careful after what happened to David. He said there was a phone box in the village where he was staying.'

'But you don't know where?' asked Harris.

'He said it was best I didn't know. I didn't argue.'

'Well, it's a start, I guess,' said Harris after she had left the room. 'I'd make sure that you have good security as well, Miss Murrell. You could be in danger too.'

'I don't need warning,' said Murrell bleakly. 'We've already had a visit. Last week. A couple of intruders broke into the office and were disturbed by the nightwatchman. One of them hit him and he's going to be off work for weeks. They left the place in a terrible mess. We assume they were looking for the manuscript.'

'I assume that you told the local police that?' said Harris.

'We said that we assumed they were after money. Like I say, the less people who know about the book the better.'

'I've had just about enough of this,' exclaimed Harris. 'If you don't begin to co-operate, I'll have you charged with obstruction. See where your non-disclosure agreement gets you then.'

'If it helps, it's not about Midas.'

'It's not?'

'No.'

Harris thought for a few moments then resolved to give voice to an idea that had been forming for a while.

'So, I'm guessing that it's about events in Germany in the mid-eighties then?' he said.

Gallagher looked at his boss in surprise and the effect on Murrell was dramatic. The publisher stared at the inspector in amazement.

'How the–' she began.

'Never mind that,' said Harris. Her reaction had emboldened him and his voice was hard-edged as he pressed home his advantage. 'There's no point in clinging onto your secret now.'

Murrell thought for a few moments then nodded in defeat.

'I suppose not,' she said. 'But if you already knew, why didn't you say?'

'We wanted to give you the chance to volunteer the information,' replied Harris. 'It helps if we know how trustworthy a person is. However, I'll level with you, we don't know all the story so we would like you to fill in the gaps.'

'And if I don't?'

'Then we'll come back with a warrant and tear this office apart,' said Harris.

'I seem to have run out of options,' said Murrell with a sigh. 'Either the villains do it or you do it.'

'It can be a fine line sometimes,' said Harris with a thin smile.

'Clearly,' said Murrell. 'You're right about the story happening in the mid-eighties in West Germany, Chief Inspector. David had been after the man at the heart of it for well over a year and had finally managed to track him down. He wouldn't tell me where he found him, though.'

'We know that bit and we also suspect that he may have turned to murder to keep his whereabouts secret. We don't know his name, though.'

'It's Simon Jones,' said Murrell. 'I don't know all the details – David said he was working on a couple of new angles – but as for Jones being a murderer, I wouldn't be surprised, given the circles in which he moved.'

'Time to tell us everything you know,' said Harris.

Half an hour later, the detectives walked out into the street and, once they were away from the building, Gallagher gave his boss an admiring look.

'Wow!' he exclaimed. 'That was one hell of a guess, guv.'

'Less of the guessing, Matty lad,' said Harris. However, he did not seem offended at the comment. Rather, he had an expression of intense satisfaction on his face. 'It's too much of a coincidence that the man at Hillview Cottage vanished at the same time David Stabler was killed. The two events had to be connected.'

'And the shaven-headed men? Where do they fit into things?'

'They could well be Midas's goons,' said Harris. 'There could be all sorts of people trying to find out what's in that book.'

The inspector's phone rang.

'Jack,' said Gina Jeffers's voice. 'Just to let you know that the Press Office has just received a call from *The Daily News*. They've found out that our body is David Stabler. They plan to run it as a front page exclusive tomorrow morning and post it online later tonight. Can I confirm it?'

'They'll run the story even if we don't,' said Harris. 'OK, go ahead.'

'Will do,' said Jeffers. 'It does mean that there'll be a media circus tomorrow, of course.'

'Delightful,' said Harris. He ended the call and slipped the phone back into his jacket pocket.

'Trouble?' asked Gallagher.

'*The Daily News* has got hold of the story.'

'Ah.'

While Gallagher hailed a cab to take them to the Indian restaurant and their meeting with Danny Mahler, the inspector made a call.

'CID squad room, please,' he said. 'DC Orr, if she's there. Hello, Sally? You getting anywhere with the German newspapers?'

'Trying to, guv, but it's slow work. It would help if we knew what we were looking for.'

'Well, allow me to narrow things down for you then,' said Harris. 'Try Dusseldorf 1984.'

'What am I looking for?'

'The murder of a prison guard.'

## Chapter fourteen

'So, what's your thinking?' asked Danny Mahler. The detective constable, a burly, bearded man dressed in an open-necked shirt and jeans, spooned curry onto his plate and tore off a piece of naan bread. 'Are you still looking at Midas for your murder?'

'Things have moved on,' said Harris. 'To be kept in these four walls, he might not be the only one in the frame.'

It was just before 5:30pm and the Levton Bridge detectives were sitting with the Metropolitan Officer in a small Indian restaurant situated in a back street not far from Euston Station. They were the only diners apart from a young couple who sat at a table in the window and were engrossed only in each other.

'So, who else are you looking at?' asked Mahler.

Gallagher glanced at Harris, who nodded.

'A guy who lives near the place where we found the body and who's gone missing,' said the sergeant. He shovelled a mouthful of curry into his mouth. 'This is excellent, Danny. We've got a curry house in Levton Bridge but it's nowhere near as good as this. They seem to think that it's enough to drown everything in sauce. We're not discounting the idea that Midas's men were after our victim, mind. Someone attacked Stabler a few weeks back and they were probably the guys who did the nightwatchman at Sudden Death Books.'

'I've not heard about that,' said Mahler. He nodded several times as Gallagher told him about the break-in. 'Yeah, sounds like them.'

'Trouble is,' said Harris, 'according to the publisher, Midas doesn't feature in the book.'

'Ah, but Midas doesn't know that, does he?' Mahler tore off another piece of naan bread and dipped it into his curry. 'And once he gets an idea into his head, he can get pretty paranoid.'

'Which is why we still need to talk to him,' said Harris. 'What's the best way to arrange it, Danny?'

'It won't be easy.' Mahler frowned. 'He knows how to play the game. He's surrounded himself with smart lawyers, who will tie you in legal knots for months. That's assuming that you even…'

The constable's voice tailed off as two shaven-headed men dressed in black entered the Indian restaurant.

'Oh-oh,' he said in a low voice. 'We got trouble. Correction, we got *big* trouble.'

The detectives watched as the larger of the new arrivals ushered the frightened young couple out of the restaurant, flipped the "Open" sign on the door to "Closed" and ordered the waiter to go into the back office.

'Midas's men?' asked Harris.

'The weasely one is Lee Garritt,' said Mahler. He sounded nervous. 'Your guy with the bad breath. The big fella with the broken nose is Max Rodney. The ex-boxer. Let me do the talking and don't try anything stupid, yeah?'

'Depends what you think is stupid,' said Harris.

Mahler looked worried, as did Gallagher. Leckie had told him stories about Harris confronting gangland hard men during his time in Manchester and the sergeant suspected that a couple of heavies trying it on was unlikely to unduly concern his boss. There was tension in the air as Garritt walked over to the detectives' table.

'What can I do for you, Lee?' asked Mahler. He tried to sound calm. 'We're just having a quiet meal. We don't want any trouble.'

'Too late for that,' said Garritt. He leered at the Levton Bridge detectives. 'These the two sheep-shaggers who have been asking questions about Midas?'

Before Mahler could reply, Harris took another mouthful of curry.

'You're right, Danny,' he said calmly. 'This *is* good.'

The inspector glanced past Garritt at Max Rodney, who had stationed himself by the door.

'However, I don't appreciate it being disturbed,' continued the inspector. 'And I'd quite like chummy to move – he's blocking out the light and I quite like to see what I'm eating.'

Mahler looked even more nervous, Gallagher tried to stop his leg shaking and Lee Garritt appeared unsure as to how to react. He was not accustomed to being spoken to like that. His unease grew as Harris took a swig of lager then stood up – the inspector was a big man.

'And I don't appreciate being called a sheep-shagger,' said Harris in a voice that was now laced with menace. 'So, if you know what's good for you, you'll let us finish our meal in peace so that we can catch our train.'

'You ain't going to catch no train,' said Garritt. He tried to sound confident but his voice lacked conviction.

'Actually, I think we are,' said Harris. 'But before we do, I'd like to know what you and Mr Muscles were doing searching David Stabler's bedsit in Sheffield?'

'That ain't none of your business,' said Garritt. He bunched his right fist.

The movement was not lost on Harris.

'I'd advise that you don't try any funny business,' said the inspector. He sat down again. 'I've dealt with more scumbags like you than you've had hot dinners. Talking of which, I'd like to finish this one, please. It's rather pleasant.'

Garritt glanced round at Max Rodney, who shrugged. This was not how encounters normally went.

'Listen, pal,' said Garritt. He was acutely conscious that he was losing face, something that he could not afford to do in London's cut-throat underworld. 'Midas wants you to stop prying into things that ain't your business.'

'Let him tell me that to my face then,' said Harris.

'Midas don't see cops.'

'If he's sensible, he'll see me.' Harris took another mouthful of curry and winked at Gallagher. 'You're right, Matty lad, it's the sauce that makes it.'

'Listen, pal–!' said Garritt.

He raised his fist to strike the inspector but did not even feel the blow as it slammed into his face and sent him crashing backwards to tumble over a next table before lying unconscious on the floor, blood pouring from his mouth. Harris walked over and looked down at him.

'That's for the nightwatchman,' he said. The inspector took a step towards the startled Max Rodney. 'Want to try to stop me finishing my tea as well, sunbeam? Before you answer that, you might like to know that I was trained by a couple of SAS lads when I was in the Army. They'd never even heard of the Queensbury Rules.'

Rodney looked at Garritt for a few moments and shook his head; he'd never seen him laid out like that – no one had dared to even try.

'Good lad,' said Harris. Garritt gave a feeble groan. 'Now, get him out of here, will you? Blood does rather tend to spoil my appetite.'

Rodney hauled his friend to his feet and helped him to the door, Garritt staggering on unsteady legs that gave way more than once.

'And tell Midas that I want to see him,' said Harris. 'He knows where to find me. Oh, and apologise to that young couple on your way out, will you? Then send them back in. They haven't finished their tea.'

Max Rodney glowered at him and helped Garritt out into the street. Harris gave a slight smile as he noticed the ex-boxer talk to the young couple, who returned nervously to their table.

'Don't worry,' said Harris, as they took their seats. 'They'll not trouble you again.'

Mahler stared at the inspector in disbelief as he sat down again.

'Jesus, man,' he said. 'Have you got a fucking death wish or what? No one does that to Lee Garritt.'

'Apparently, they do,' said Harris. 'Besides, you saw what happened. It was self-defence. Midas is not going to ignore us after what happened here, is he?'

'He certainly isn't,' said Mahler. 'He hates being shown up.'

The Met officer glanced nervously towards the door.

'However, for now,' he said, 'and I hope you don't take this the wrong way, Jack, might I suggest that we settle the bill and you fuck off back up north?'

Harris gave a slight smile, finished the last of his lager and stood up. Gallagher sighed with relief and the detectives left the restaurant and went their separate ways, Mahler gratefully heading back to his office, constantly glancing over his shoulder as he did so, and the Levton Bridge detectives to Euston Station. Soon, they were sitting in the train as it waited to depart. Gallagher, who had spoken little, looked out of the window and noticed to his alarm that two other men in black were standing on the platform and staring at them. Harris noticed them as well.

'Making sure that we go back to the sheep, Matty lad,' he said.

'You do push your luck sometimes.'

Harris did not reply and the sergeant only started to relax when the train pulled out of the station and began the long journey north, rumbling past familiar landmarks that he had greeted with such joy just a few hours previously but which he now viewed with relief as they disappeared from view behind him.

# Chapter fifteen

Jack Harris was up early the next morning and only the faintest streaks of light heralded the approach of dawn as he and the dogs left the cottage for their morning walk. Harris had lived half-way up Dead Hill for several years, having stumbled across the house on a Sunday afternoon walk not long after moving back to the valley. Having spent many hours overseeing the cottage's renovation, he had eventually moved in, immediately relishing the fact that, when he looked out of the living room window across the fields, he could not see any signs of human beings, no farmhouses, no cottages, no barns. Indeed, he rarely saw anyone, apart from the odd hiker and occasionally the shepherd on his quad bike with his dog perched on the back of the vehicle. As with Simon Jones at Hillview Cottage, the inspector felt for most of the time when he was at home as if he were the last man alive. It was an irony not lost on him.

Nor had he overlooked the fact that he and David Stabler had shared a love of the hills as well. It was a fine line between different sides of the same story, thought the inspector as he and the two dogs headed off across the fields, the animals hardly requiring the detective's torch beam to guide their way as they followed well-trodden paths.

On their return to the cottage, Harris gave the dogs something to eat, dropped some bread into the toaster and switched on the kettle. He had just sat down to his breakfast at the kitchen table when his mobile phone rang.

'Sorry to ring you so early, Jack,' said Gina Jeffers. Harris could hear the sound of a car engine in the background. 'But the media circus has read the piece in *The Daily News* and is descending on Levton Bridge. I'm on the way there now.'

'I'll not be long,' said Harris. 'What does the article say?'

'Not a lot. They clearly don't know much more than his name, so they've padded it out with background about him.'

'Does it mention the book?' asked Harris. He took a mouthful of toast.

'Just that it is believed that he was writing one. They would not appear to know what it's about or who's publishing it.'

'I take it that you will want me to make a statement when I arrive at the nick?'

'I think it would be a good idea,' said Jeffers. 'It might stop the Press Office phones ringing off the hook, if nothing else.'

'OK, will do.' Harris ended the call and looked at the dogs. 'And so it begins. If we're not careful, we could lose control of this one. Too many journalists digging around.'

Having loaded the animals into the back of the Land Rover, the inspector drove the few miles to Levton Bridge where he was greeted by a large number of journalists in front of the police station. Having parked – Curtis had never liked the inspector taking one of the spaces at the front of the building so he always left the vehicle there – Harris removed the dogs from the vehicle and they followed him up the steps, ignoring the journalists' shouted questions. At the top, he nodded a greeting to Jeffers and turned to face the media scrum.

'DCI Harris will answer your questions now,' shouted Jeffers. She pointed to a radio reporter. 'Yes, Jake, your question, please.'

'Is the story in *The News* true?' shouted the reporter. 'Has David Stabler been murdered?'

The gathering fell quiet.

'I can confirm that his body was found at a remote location in the valley, yes,' said Harris. 'We wanted to delay releasing anything until we were sure of his identity.'

'Then how come *The News* found out first?' shouted another reporter.

'You'd have to ask them,' said Harris. 'However, I can confirm that the article is correct when it says he was shot dead and that we have launched a murder investigation.'

'Do you have anyone in custody?' shouted a radio reporter.

'Not at this stage. However, I can confirm that we are pursuing several leads of interest.'

'David Stabler specialised in organised crime,' said a newspaper reporter. 'Do you believe that he was killed because of something he had written?'

'I'd rather not say.'

'Can you confirm that he was writing a book?' asked another journalist. 'Was that why he was murdered?'

'I would rather that you refrain from speculation.'

'Then perhaps you'd like to give us more information,' said a reporter. 'That way we wouldn't need to speculate.'

Harris opted to ignore the comment.

'Any more questions?' he asked. 'Because, as I am sure you can appreciate, I am very busy.'

'Do you think that any other journalists are in danger?' asked a reporter.

'It's difficult to say,' replied Harris. He let his gaze roam round the gathering. 'However, as I have said to you many times, the manner in which you report things can have a significant impact. With that in mind, I am sure that you will report the unfortunate death of Mr Stabler responsibly.'

A low murmuring ran through the assembled journalists. Jeffers frowned; this was not going well.

'Are you saying that he–' began a journalist.

'I have no further comment to make at this stage.' Harris turned and pushed his way into the reception area, followed by the dogs. 'Talk to the Press Office if you want anything else.'

Jeffers followed him into the building.

'Not helpful, Jack,' she said when they were out of earshot of the journalists. 'The last thing we need to do is antagonise them.'

'Well, what do you expect?' said Harris. He punched in the code on the security door and pushed his way into the rear of the building. 'They have to realise that this needs to be reported with care.'

'Yes, but–'

'Listen, Gina,' said Harris. He turned to face her with a fierce expression on his face. 'It is highly likely that David Stabler did lose his life over something he was writing. And James Cronin may well be in danger for the same reason unless we can get to him first. Journalists have to realise that they need to be accountable for what they write.'

Jeffers watched him in unhappy silence as he strode up the stairs, dogs at his heels. She knew that there was little point in remonstrating with him in this mood. Still brooding over his encounter with the reporters, the inspector spent the next half an hour in his office and had just poured water from a plastic bottle into the dogs' bowls then switched on his kettle when Philip Curtis walked into the room. The commander scowled when he saw the animals but said nothing and instead shut the office door and sat down at the desk.

'That looks ominous,' said Harris. He held up the tea caddy. 'Brew?'

'Er, no thanks, Jack.'

Harris dropped a tea bag into a mug.

'So, what can I do you for?' he asked.

'Gina told me what you said to the journalists out there. I'm not sure that was the right way to go about things.'

'It had to be said. The last thing we want is a media free-for-all, especially if there's someone out there with a grudge against journalists.'

'I appreciate that, Jack, but we need them on our side and we also need to remember that they're probably frightened at the thought of someone killing one of their own.'

'I guess,' said Harris but he did not sound convinced.

'However, that's not why I am here,' said Curtis. 'Would you care to explain why I have just had an irate detective chief inspector on from the Met, playing merry hell about one of my officers allegedly assaulting someone in an Indian restaurant?'

'He made the first move.'

'So, it's true then?'

'All we were doing was having a meal with a Met colleague, when this Garritt fellow butted in.' Harris poured the hot water into the mug. 'I merely defended myself.'

'Merely defended yourself? He spent the night in hospital with concussion and four fewer teeth than he started the day with!'

Harris stopped stirring his tea and turned round to face the commander.

'I'm sorry,' he said. 'But he tried to intimidate us into dropping our inquiries into Francis Jacques and I don't play that game. Particularly not when Midas is one of our suspects for the murder of David Stabler.'

'Well, the Met DCI says that, if there's an official complaint, he'll not be able to brush it under the carpet. I keep telling you, Jack, London's different to this place. You can't go throwing your weight around like you do up here.'

'I know, I know.' Harris placed his mug of tea on the desk and sat down. 'Maybe I overstepped the mark.'

'I'm sure that Lee Garritt's dentist would agree.'

'Not if Garritt goes private, he won't.'

'For God's sake, man, this is serious! This could get you into all sorts of trouble. Anyway, hopefully the complaint will not come to anything. I take it all this means that Midas is your main suspect for the murder?'

'At the very least, he has got questions to answer,' said Harris.

'It would certainly appear so and it all sounds more promising than this chap at Hillview Cottage? Simon Jones, is it? I mean, where does he fit into things?'

'I'm not sure yet,' said Harris. 'Maybe he doesn't.'

There was a knock on the office door.

'Come in,' said Harris.

Sally Orr walked into the room; the young constable's eyes gleamed with excitement.

'You won the lottery?' asked Harris.

'As good as,' she said. 'See, I've just been going through the overnight emails and we've been sent something that you'll want to see. I've just forwarded it to you.'

Harris tapped into his emails on his desktop computer.

'You'll need to open the attachment,' said Orr. 'It's not great quality, I am afraid.'

'What is it?' asked Curtis.

'It's a scan from one of the English-speaking newspapers published in Germany in the mid-eighties,' said Orr. 'A local library assistant found it for us.'

As the scan slowly revealed itself, Roberts and Gallagher walked into the office and joined Curtis in staring over the inspector's shoulder as he leaned forward to peer closer at the grainy newspaper cutting. Orr watched them with unalloyed joy – as the newest recruit to the team, she always felt acutely the need to prove herself and knew that what she had found would prove to be a dramatic intervention. What the scan revealed was the front page of a newspaper that bore a photograph of a prison van with its rear doors wide open, beneath a headline stating "Break Out!" There was a subsidiary headline, "Prison guard shot dead", and at the bottom of the page was a police photograph of a sallow, dark-haired, clean-shaven man with eyes that seemed to glint with a sense of amusement. Harris and the others leaned closer and studied the image with intense interest.

'Is that…?' asked Harris.

'Sure is.' Sally Orr beamed. 'Meet Simon Jones.'

Harris stared into Jones's eyes, fascinated by the face of a man who had so far remained elusive to the investigation team. For all the inspector had rebuked his team for utterances that added to the sense of mystery surrounding Jones, he had begun to wonder if the police had fallen victim to some kind of elaborate hoax. Now Simon Jones was real.

*The prison van left the police station in Dusseldorf shortly after 2:00pm and slotted into the light early afternoon city centre traffic. Sitting alone in the back of the vehicle was Simon Jones, who had been arrested the previous week following a series of police raids, the culmination of an operation that had been meticulously planned by detectives over several months. The arrests had been carried out by a police team that had been assembled to investigate a gang suspected of carrying out numerous armed robberies on banks. Although nineteen people had been arrested, many were minor players and detectives were mainly interested in four of them – the ringleaders. Simon Jones was one of the four, the gang's strategist, the brains behind their activities. He had that morning been questioned for several hours by senior detectives and was now being taken back to prison to await his next court appearance the following day. As the vehicle gathered pace,*

*Jones was a picture of nervous energy, glancing repeatedly towards the back door.*

*The van had been under way for a little over five minutes when the traffic slowed for a red light at a major intersection. As it did so, Jones heard the squeal of tyres as a car cut in front of the van at high speed, forcing the driver to curse and jam down hard on the brakes. As the vehicle juddered to a halt, a masked man armed with a sub-machine gun leapt out of the cars and Jones heard shouting. There was a loud bang and the van's rear doors were wrenched open. Jones reacted quickly, jumping out and starting to run across the road in the opposite direction from the waiting car. The masked man shouted and gestured with his gun towards the vehicle but Jones kept going. The gunman pointed towards the car again but, as he did so, a prison guard appeared round the corner of the van. The gunman gave a cry of alarm and his weapon spat bullets. The guard sunk to his knees then pitched forward and lay still, blood welling from a wound to his stomach.*

*For a second, there was no sound, as if the whole scene were being filmed in slow motion, then the cacophony started up again as terrified bystanders watched the drama unfold and the gunman stared at the mortally wounded guard before whirling round to identify Jones among the crowd. Failing to do so, he gave a furious yell and ran back to the getaway car, pointing his gun at anyone who threatened to get too close. Once he had hurled himself into the passenger seat, the masked driver rammed his foot on the accelerator and the car sped from the scene with its tyres squealing and engine roaring. Within seconds, the air was filled with the wail of sirens. Of Simon Jones there was no sign.*

'Good, eh?' said Gallagher. 'Explains why he's been running for the best part of forty years.'

'Indeed it does,' said Harris. He glanced at Sally Orr. 'Good work, Constable. Good work indeed.'

'I had help,' said Orr. She tried to come over as professional but could not contain her delight at the inspector's comment.

'And you're sure that Simon Jones is the man at Hillview Cottage, are you?' said Curtis as he returned to his seat.

'It would explain a lot if he was,' said Harris. 'Like Matty says, no wonder he's gone to all that trouble to hide his whereabouts. They go to all that trouble to spring him from prison and he legs it. It's enough to lead to some fairly pointed questions from his fellow gang members, not to mention the police and the prison service.'

'I assume that's what the book is about?' asked Curtis.

'That's what the publisher told us yesterday,' said Harris. 'Stabler planned to tell the gang's story and end the book by revealing that he had tracked Jones down. Finding him was his big scoop.'

'And motive enough for Jones to kill him,' said Gallagher.

'But is it?' asked Curtis. 'I mean, it was forty years ago, Matthew. Would anyone really be that interested today? The other gang members must be pretty old themselves now. Some of them may even be dead.'

'But I'm guessing not all of them, sir, and in my experience, criminals have very long memories. And even if they are dead, the police will still want to talk to him, won't they?'

'I suppose so,' said Curtis.

'Anyway, it's a start,' said Harris. He looked at the commander. 'I'm going to take up your suggestion about seeing the new head of Special Branch. See if she's prepared to fill in some of the gaps now that we know so much of the story.'

'Good idea,' replied Curtis. 'I want us all to be on the same page on this one.'

'And we'll keep digging up more stuff on the gang,' said Roberts. She glanced at Orr, who nodded. 'It should get easier now that we know what we're dealing with.'

'Just steer clear of anything official for now,' said Harris. 'At least until we know what the Germans are up to.'

Roberts looked as if she was going to say something but before she could speak, there was a knock on the door and Gina Jeffers walked in. The press officer was clutching a sheaf of papers.

'Some of the early reports about the murder that have just gone online,' she said. 'I'm afraid your warning about speculation fell on deaf ears, Jack.'

She placed the computer print-outs on the desk.

'They're casting around for anything to bulk up their reports,' she said. 'Several of them have mentioned the story that David wrote about Midas's wife and suggesting that the book might be about him.'

'He'll not like that,' said Gallagher.

'He certainly won't,' said Harris. His desk phone rang and he picked up the receiver. 'Hello, DCI Harris.'

'It's the Control Room, sir,' said a woman's voice. 'I have a call for you from a solicitor who says that he represents a man called Francis Jacques. Should I put him through?'

'Sure.' Harris covered the receiver with his hand. 'Midas's solicitor.'

'That didn't take long,' said Gallagher.

There was a click on the line and Harris heard a cultured voice.

'DCI Harris?'

'Speaking.' The inspector put the call on speaker.

'My name is Jeremy Rowley. I am Francis Jacques's lawyer. Apparently, you would like to talk to my client? Or at least that's what we were told by one of his associates in between him spitting out broken teeth.'

'I certainly would,' replied Harris. 'However, if yesterday's performance is anything to go by, it would seem that he is somewhat reluctant to engage with us.'

'On this occasion, he is prepared to make an exception,' said Rowley. 'He is aware of certain – how can we describe it? – unfortunate references to him in the media in connection with the death of David Stabler. He is somewhat alarmed at the effect on his reputation of such idle speculation.'

'Well, they didn't get it from us.'

'I am sure that Mr Jacques will be gratified to hear it,' replied Rowley. 'But, nevertheless, he would still like to meet you in order to clear up any misunderstandings that may have occurred. How does two o'clock tomorrow sound?'

'Fine. Will he be coming here?'

'Mr Jacques rarely ventures outside of London, I am afraid, and would rather that you meet him down here. Perhaps you would like to come to his office?'

'I think that somewhere neutral might be more preferable?' said Harris. 'Not that I don't trust your client, of course, but I don't imagine that Lee Garritt will be pleased to see me again, do you?'

'I very much doubt it. Very well, I'll book a room in a hotel close to Euston Station. Can I ask if you will be attending on your own?'

'Detective Sergeant Gallagher will be accompanying me.'

'Ah, the estimable Sergeant Gallagher,' said Rowley. 'It will be good to make his acquaintance, given what we have heard about him. I will get back to you with the details later in the day.'

The line went dead and Harris replaced the receiver and gave a wry smile.

'Well, Gina,' he said, looking at the press officer. 'It seems that I was wrong about the dangers of media speculation. On this occasion, it would appear to have smoked out our Mr Jacques. We've clearly got him worried.'

Harris gave the sergeant an impish look.

'And he seems very keen to meet you, Matty lad,' he said.

Gallagher gave his boss a sick look.

'Ruin my day, why don't you?' he said.

## Chapter sixteen

'So, ladies and gentlemen,' said Harris as he scanned the faces in the briefing room at Levton Bridge Police Station later that morning. 'I think it's time that we started to make sense of things before myself and Matty go back to London tomorrow. Needless to say, anything discussed stays within this room. I don't want it to find its way to any journalists.'

The inspector turned to the large noticeboard on the wall behind him. Not for the first time during the inquiry, he was struck by how sparse the material that had been pinned up appeared to be. Normally in complex murder investigations, there would be numerous faces by this stage of proceedings, suspects, victims and possibly witnesses, each one with the links drawn in between them. However, on this occasion, there were just two faces, the grainy image of Simon Jones and a police mug shot of a man in his early thirties with spiky brown hair and pock-marked cheeks.

'As it stands, we have two main suspects for the murder of David Stabler,' said Harris. He tapped the police mugshot. 'Francis Jacques, aka Midas, who believed that Stabler was writing a book about him, and Simon Jones, an

English criminal operating in West Germany in the 1980s who is the actual subject. Both would seem to have strong motives for the book not to appear.'

'I thought Midas was older,' said Gillian Roberts. She was sitting on the front row. 'When was that picture taken?'

'Long enough ago to be largely useless,' said Gallagher. 'It dates from the last time he was arrested, in fact. Thirteen years ago when the cops pulled him in after a warehouse security guard was shot. They had to let him go for lack of evidence – a familiar story when it comes to Midas.'

'Do they not have anything more recent?' asked Roberts.

'They do, yes,' said Gallagher. 'Loads of it. Midas is one of their top targets and they carry out regular surveillance to keep up with the members of his entourage.'

'So why don't we have one of those pictures then?' asked Roberts.

'Inter-force politics,' said Gallagher. 'Danny Mahler says that his governor is unwilling to co-operate with us after what happened at the curry house.'

'But aren't we all on the same side?' asked Alison Butterfield. The young detective constable looked round at the others. 'Surely, they are as keen as we are to see Midas locked up?'

'According to Danny, their top brass are not impressed that we have persuaded Midas to talk to us,' said Gallagher. 'They've been trying for years and now here we are, a couple of woolyback cops coming onto their patch and making them look stupid. Woolyback is the word Danny's governor used, not mine.'

'And not the first time we've heard it,' said Harris. He looked round the room.

'If you ask me, Stabler's murder has got nothing to with Midas,' said Roberts. 'No one round here has seen his men.'

Harris tapped the print-out of the German newspaper cutting that had been pinned up on the noticeboard.

'If that's the case,' he said, 'it would leave us with Simon Jones as our prime suspect. Have we been able to find out anything more about him?'

'Just what we've been able to glean from the newspapers,' said Roberts. 'Sally's got something to make the board look a bit more loved, haven't you?'

'I have,' said Orr.

The constable's eyes gleamed – she was relishing once more being able to occupy centre stage as she held up another print-out of a newspaper cutting, this time bearing the image of Simon Jones and three swarthy men, each of whom stared at the camera in sullen fashion.

'Simon Jones was major league,' she said. 'Part of a gang which was responsible for a string of armed robberies in the early eighties across what was then West Germany. He and the other three lovelies were the ringleaders. They're all German, career criminals with long records.'

'What kind of robberies did they commit?' asked Harris.

'Banks and factory payrolls, mainly. One bank teller was shot dead and another was blinded in one eye when they smashed through a counter window. It took the German police months to gather enough evidence but eventually they arrested nineteen men in early 1984. They were jailed for terms of between six and twenty-five years. Jones was sentenced to thirteen years in his absence.'

Gillian Roberts took the cutting from the constable and pinned it onto the noticeboard.

'There, that looks a bit better,' she said. She stood back to admire her handiwork then frowned. 'However, we haven't been able to establish a definite link with David Stabler's death. We don't even know if the others are still alive. I know you don't want us to ring the police in Dusseldorf, Hawk, but it would save us a lot of time and effort.'

'You might be able to do it after I've seen Special Branch this afternoon.'

'Fair enough,' said Roberts. 'I suppose.'

Harris gave her a look but did not pursue the point and instead returned his attention to the gaps on the noticeboard.

'I can't help thinking that we're missing something,' he said. The inspector looked at Alistair Marshall. 'Have we found out anything more about the other articles that Stabler had written?'

'Loads,' said the detective constable. He held up a sheaf of articles that he had printed out from media websites. 'We found twenty-eight pieces written by him for national newspapers in the past year, plus half a dozen that appeared in *The Organisation*.'

'Anyone who might be upset about what he had written?' asked Harris.

'Take your pick,' said Marshall. He flicked through the pages. 'Gangs in London, gangs in Manchester, including some you probably dealt with in Manchester, the Triads, the Mafia, South American drug dealers, Middle Eastern gun runners, African people traffickers. You name it, David Stabler wrote about it.'

Harris looked at the noticeboard again, this time focusing on a photograph of the tent at Haggs Scarr.

'Any luck tracking down James Cronin?' he asked.

'Afraid not,' said Gallagher. 'The last time his mobile phone was switched on, he was in Leeds, but when the local cops checked out the address for us, the neighbours said they hadn't seen him for a couple of days. One of them said they saw him loading a couple of bags into his car like he was in a hurry.'

'Well, we've got to find him and find him quickly,' said Harris. 'Before someone else does.'

# Chapter seventeen

James Cronin sat in the cramped living room of the cottage and stared at the screen on his laptop. He had written so many words since arriving in the Yorkshire Dales two days previously that they seemed to swim before his eyes. The task of finishing Stabler's book had become an obsession and one that was taking its toll on him. It had become all too real when Heather Murrell rang him to tell him that Stabler was dead and, ever since arriving at the cottage, he had increasingly been imagining things, fancying that he could hear voices in the road or someone trying the back door. There was never anyone there when he checked but he was determined to deliver the final manuscript as quickly as possible.

Cronin glanced at the wall clock – hopefully, his man would be as good as his word and turn up. Things would be easier if he was prepared to fill in the final gaps in the story. His mind went back to Stabler, who had phoned him several weeks previously to suggest working together. Cronin was surprised; he hardly knew the man – the only time they ever met was on the rare occasions that Stabler deigned to attend police press conferences and, even then, he had always given the impression that he held fellow journalists in low regard. They'd met in a pub in Leeds where Stabler had handed him a memory stick containing the manuscript to date, a series of background notes and a bag of photocopied newspaper articles. *It was the last time Cronin heard from him.*

Now, he glanced at the clock again. His visitor was due in a half an hour. His mind went back to the days that followed the meeting with Stabler. Initially, Cronin had read through the notes and the draft manuscript more out of interest than in the belief that he would actually become involved. However, as he read, he became increasingly excited about the potential. After so much failure in his career, Cronin could see that, here, finally, was a chance to make his name and prove that people like Heather Murrell were wrong about him. Despite himself, Cronin found himself almost wishing that some harm might befall Stabler. Rebuking himself for the idea, he instead developed a plan to persuade Stabler to allow him a credit as joint author.

Several weeks passed without contact from Stabler then Murrell rang to tell him that Stabler was dead. Trying to conceal his shock, Cronin had forced his fear to the back of his mind and reminded the publisher about his pledge to finish the book. That Murrell did not sound enthusiastic only hardened Cronin's resolve and eventually she agreed. She knew that she had no alternative; he was the only other person with the notes and the memory stick.

After ending the call, Cronin had booked the cottage, somewhere he occasionally brought girlfriends, hurriedly packed a bag and left his home. Now, he stood up and walked into the kitchen, opening a cupboard from which he took a half-empty bottle of whisky and a glass. He glanced at the wall clock: 1:30pm.

'Bit early, James,' he murmured. 'But who's to know?'

As he began to pour the drink, he heard a noise and, cursing himself for leaving the front door open, walked quickly back into the living room to see a man standing in the doorway that led from the hallway.

'Jesus!' he exclaimed. 'You gave me a shock. You're early. I wasn't sure if you'd turn up what with…'

Cronin's voice tailed off as the man produced a handgun from under his jacket and pointed it at him.

'*You*!' gasped Cronin. '*You* killed David!'

'I had to,' said the man. 'I can't let the story be told. I told Stabler that, but he wouldn't listen. If he had, he would be alive today.'

Cronin stood motionless for a few moments then turned quickly and darted into the kitchen where he lunged for the back door handle. The man followed him and pulled the trigger.

* * *

Charlie Bourne was sitting in his office at force headquarters when the desk phone rang.

'Charlie?' said a voice. 'Josef Haller.'

The Special Branch officer gave a slight sigh; it was the third time that Haller had contacted him over the past forty-eight hours. 'Any news?'

'Like I keep telling you, I'll contact you when I have something.'

'I know, but I wanted to check something. I've been reading the media reports of the investigation into David Stabler's murder and they make no mention of Simon. I take it that means that Harris and his team still do not know about him?'

'I'm not sure what they know, Josef, but from what I hear, they're still interested in the man at Hillview Cottage.'

'I thought you were going to dissuade them from such an unwise course of action.' There was an edge to Haller's voice now. 'Besides, I assumed from the media reports that they are more interested in this London gang leader. Midas, is it? The reports seem to suggest that the book is about him.'

'Yes, but I don't know the exact–'

'Will Jack Harris not tell you?'

'He doesn't like people interfering with his investigations, Josef. However, from what I gather, no one has seen the manuscript, not even the publisher.'

'Well, if Harris has got it into his head that it's something to do with Jones, we need to make sure that he stays away from him,' said Haller. 'Otherwise, he risks jeopardising our investigation, which is at a very delicate stage. You need to make that clear to him. If he knows where Simon Jones is, he must tell me.'

'We're seeing him a bit later. I'll make the point again. That's the best I can do, but I can tell you what he'll say. He'll say that it's all very well making these demands but that he's heard nothing to persuade him to co-operate.'

There was silence for a few moments.

'You still there?' asked Bourne.

'I'm still here,' said Haller. 'Look, I'm about to take a big risk, Charlie. Maybe Jack Harris *does* need to know why Simon Jones is of such interest to us. You see, he and his team have stumbled onto something so sensitive that very few people over here even know about it…'

# Chapter eighteen

After leaving the briefing, Jack Harris made the hour's journey from Levton Bridge down to the lowlands and the selection of 1960s buildings that comprised force headquarters. The inspector brought the Land Rover to a halt in the wooded car park and walked with purpose towards the building that included the Special Branch offices. Jack Harris was a man on a mission, a man determined to regain control of the situation. Soon, he was sitting in a second floor office staring across the desk at a slim woman with short dark hair and wearing a sharp business suit.

Harris had heard a lot about Detective Chief Inspector Janet Maynard in the three weeks since she had transferred from North Yorkshire. He knew that she was a sharp, no-nonsense character who was good at her job and not afraid to confront people, regardless of their reputation. Maynard, for her part, eyed him warily; she'd heard all the stories of a man who regarded his CID division as his own personal fiefdom where the only law was the law according to Jack Harris. However, she had decided not to judge him on water cooler tittle-tattle. Speak as you find, had always been one of her favourite mantras.

The third person present was Charlie Bourne, who was feeling acutely uncomfortable, concerned at the way Harris would react if he suspected that Special Branch had been passing on too much information to the Germans. Despite his unease, Bourne watched Maynard and Harris with a sense of anticipation; everyone in the force had been looking forward to the first encounter between the two senior officers. Irresistible force meets immovable object, they said. It was not an outcome that anyone would like to predict. Maynard began the conversation.

'It's good to meet you, Jack,' she said. 'I've heard a lot about you.'

'Likewise, Janet,' said Harris. 'I was going to come to see you anyway but it would seem that our hands are being forced by circumstances.'

'Yes, I'm sorry about that.' Maynard was determined to keep the conversation civil, if at all possible. 'The last thing I want is for there to be friction between us. I have too much respect for you to allow that to happen.'

Harris inclined his head slightly. Smooth, he thought. Diplomatic. He appreciated the gesture, even if he was determined that it would not work.

'However,' she continued, 'I am sure you appreciate that in our line of work some things have to be handled on a need-to-know basis.'

Harris gave a slight smile. This was more his kind of game. Hardball. Janet Maynard came over as someone who liked to dictate the way situations played out and Harris relished the thought of what he was about to do. Time, he decided, to drop the bombshell.

'This need-to-know?' he asked innocently. 'Can I assume that it extends to protecting Simon Jones?'

The inspector waited for the impact. It did not take long to come as both Maynard and Bourne stared at him in amazement.

'How the…?' blurted out Bourne.

Harris gave him a hard look.

'Because, Charlie,' he said, 'when it comes to murder, it's our job to know.'

Maynard chewed her lip.

'How did you discover his name?' she asked.

'It wasn't difficult once Charlie pointed us in the right direction.'

'But I didn't tell you anything!' protested Bourne. Maynard glared at him. Now, he was under fire from both sides. 'Honest, ma'am, I didn't say anything.'

'Clearly, you said enough,' said Maynard coldly. 'However, we'll discuss this later. This is not the time or the place. Jack, this puts me in a very difficult position but it does not change the fact that I cannot–'

'Can we stop playing games!' snapped Harris. 'Simon Jones is a suspect in a murder case.'

'Yes, I appreciate that but for all we know, all you've got is the name. This could be nothing more than a fishing exercise.'

'Not quite,' said Harris with a thin smile. 'See, we know that he was part of an organised crime gang in West Germany in the mid-eighties. Dusseldorf, to be precise. We know that they specialised in armed robbery and that Jones was among nineteen men arrested by the German police in 1984. We also know that he escaped after a break-out from a prison van in which a prison guard was shot dead and we know that David Stabler had tracked him down for a book that he was writing. And for what it's worth, we don't buy the dementia thing. How am I doing so far?'

'You seem extraordinarily well informed,' said Maynard bleakly. 'Do you mind if I ask where you found this out? I hope that you didn't contact the police in Germany?'

'We haven't so far but we are quite prepared to do so, if people keep playing silly buggers with us,' said Harris. 'What I need to know is why the German police are so interested in protecting him after the best part of forty years.'

'I might be more inclined to help if the case against Jones was stronger,' said Maynard. 'It sounds pretty thin to me. The Germans certainly take that view, isn't that right, Charlie?'

Harris gave him a hard look and Bourne closed his eyes. His day was going from bad to worse.

'I'd rather that Special Branch did not go gossiping to other forces about our inquiry,' said Harris. 'If we assume that we are operating on a need-to-know basis, your pal in Germany does not need to know.'

Despite the tension, Maynard allowed herself a slight smile at the barb. Silence settled on the room for a few moments.

'So where do we go from here?' she asked. 'There are national security–'

'There are only so many times you can play that card, Janet. Besides, national security will count for nothing if I issue an appeal to the media to help us track down Simon Jones, will it? I've got a picture of him now – admittedly an old one, but it'll do the job. And don't think I won't do it. Another writer is finishing the book and we believe that he's in danger. I can't ignore that.'

Maynard glanced at Bourne.

'I take it that Jack doesn't do bluffing?' she said.

'I don't think he does, ma'am, no.'

'It seems that I have no option,' said Maynard. 'OK, tell him what you know.'

'But what about…?'

'Tell him,' repeated Maynard. She gave Harris a stern look. 'But you have to promise that this does not go out of this room. The German investigation is at a very delicate stage and a wrong move now could jeopardise many months of work – and, for the moment, we are not prepared to divulge the identity of the officer who contacted us. His work is highly sensitive.'

Harris nodded. During his time heading up the gangs initiative in Manchester, he'd protected the identity of enough officers to argue the point.

'Fair enough,' he said. 'So, what's the story, Charlie?'

'Our contact has told us that Simon Jones is still active and part of a gang that has developed links with far-right terrorist groupings operating out of Germany. The word is that several recent bank robberies were carried out to fund planned attacks across Europe. The Germans are ready to move against them and that's why they are being so cagey.'

'But Simon Jones must be in his seventies by now.'

'Nevertheless, the German police believe that he remains a skilled strategist,' said Bourne. 'They do not buy the dementia thing, either, and they want to do a deal with him.'

'What kind of deal?'

'They want to see if he's prepared to tell them what he knows.'

'Why should he do that?' asked Harris.

'He still has a lengthy prison sentence hanging over his head. He knows that he would not survive prison, particularly after what happened to the guard, so the Germans plan to set aside the sentence if he co-operates with them.'

'Good old-fashioned blackmail,' said Harris with a curl of the lip. 'Not exactly honourable, is it?'

'They think that the ends justify the means. The only problem with the plan was that they had no idea where he was until our forensics guy triggered the alert on the fingerprint database.'

'And what happens if we find him before they do?'

Bourne glanced at Maynard but said nothing. This was top-level politics – well above his pay grade.

'If you persist with your inquiries, our contact says that the Germans will make it a national incident,' said Maynard. 'A dispute between governments with you in the middle of it – and me and Charlie, for that matter.'

'More blackmail,' said Harris.

'I'm sorry, Jack, but that's the way the game is being played,' she said.

Harris stood up.

'Not my game,' he said.

'Don't write the Germans off that quickly,' said Maynard. 'Our contact says that he can appreciate your position and would be prepared to come over to meet you, if you feel it might help. He's keen that things do not escalate.'

Harris thought for a moment, nodded and sat down again.

'It might prove useful, I suppose,' he said.

'When are you free?' asked Maynard. 'How about tomorrow?'

'I'm going to London to meet Midas tomorrow. How about the day after? Things should be clearer by then.'

'I'll check if he can make it,' said Maynard.

It was a deeply pensive Jack Harris who returned to the Land Rover a few minutes later and headed back to Levton Bridge, appreciating as ever how the lowland landscape gradually started to give way to the northern hills. Half-way there, he parked in a lay-by near to one of his favourite spots where he let the dogs out. For the best part of an hour, they explored the sparsely wooded banks of the lake and, as he walked, the inspector turned the details of his meeting with the Special Branch officers over and over in his mind. As he did so, one phrase kept coming back to him from the briefing with his officers earlier in the day. *I can't help thinking that we're missing something.*

## Chapter nineteen

The ambulance crew was already inside the cottage a mile out of Muker village in Swaledale when the first police vehicle arrived. It was 10:30am and, having parked up, the two uniformed police officers headed into the house, where they found the ambulance personnel crouched next to the body of a man lying on his front on the kitchen floor. They moved aside so that the officers could see the dried bloodstain on the man's back.

'He was dead when you arrived, I take it?' asked one of the officers.

'And had been for a number of hours,' said one of the crew.

'Who called it in?'

'Leccy man,' she said. 'Came to read the meter, got no answer and noticed that the front door was unlocked. He checked round the back and saw the body through the window.'

'Any identification on him?' asked the police officer.

'His wallet's on the table in the living room. We didn't look in it, though. Thought it best to leave it to you.'

The police officer nodded and walked back into the living room, where he pulled a driving licence out of the wallet.

'James Cronin.' He looked thoughtfully at his colleague. 'That rings a bell. Wasn't there a missing persons alert about him overnight? Something about the cops in Levton Bridge looking for him as part of a murder investigation?'

* * *

Jack Harris and Matty Gallagher were on the southbound train heading for London once more when the inspector's mobile rang.

'Gillian,' he said, taking the call. 'What news?'

'I am afraid we were too late to save James Cronin.' The detective inspector's voice sounded flat. 'Somebody got to him first.'

Harris closed his eyes.

'Where?' he asked. The inspector opened his eyes, looked across the table at Gallagher and mouthed the word 'Cronin'. Gallagher frowned but said nothing.

'The cops in North Yorkshire found his body in a cottage in the Dales,' said Roberts.

'And we're sure it's him?'

'His ID says it is and his car is parked outside,' said Roberts.

'How did he die?'

'Shot in the back,' said Roberts. 'Looks like he was trying to get away.'

'You going to send someone over there to take a look?' asked Harris.

'I thought I'd go myself. One of their DCIs is leading the investigation and I reckon it needs someone who can handle the inter-force politics.'

'Agreed,' said Harris. 'Any sign of the manuscript?'

'Not from what I can gather. There's no sign of a laptop, either. Looks like whoever killed him took it with them. Job done.'

'Any idea who the North Yorkshire DCI is?'

'A chap called Geoff Smith.'

'He went for the job that Janet Maynard got,' said Harris. 'Look, I know this goes against the grain, Gillian, but, although I'm happy for you to tell him about Midas, I don't want you to mention Jones. Not until I've met the German officer, anyway.'

'But surely I'll have to?' protested Roberts. 'I mean, he is a key part of the inquiry, is he not? If you rule out Midas today, he's our only remaining suspect, isn't he? I mean, he has as strong a motive as anyone for blocking publication. Stronger, you could argue.'

'He has,' said Harris. 'But the Germans are piling the pressure on and I need to see if the national security line holds water before I decide how to play it.'

'Well, I think you're wrong and, if anyone asks, I'll tell them so.'

'Noted.' Harris frowned. It was rare that Roberts questioned his judgement in such an outspoken way and he did not like the way that events were creating divisions within his team; it was not the way Jack Harris ran his inquiries. 'I don't like it either but just go with me for the moment, will you?'

There was silence for a few moments.

'That an order?' asked Roberts.

'It can be if you want it to be.'

'There's no need for that,' said Roberts.

'Thank you,' said Harris. He ended the call, slipped the phone back into his jacket pocket and looked at Gallagher. 'Shot dead in a cottage in the Yorkshire Dales.'

'That complicates things.'

'It certainly does.' Harris glanced at his watch. 'I think we'd better drop in on Sudden Death Books before we see Midas. Give them the happy news. Be interesting if they already know about that one as well.'

Gallagher nodded and went back to staring gloomily out of the window at the passing fields. Normally, he relished the southward journey that took him closer to his former home but the thought of meeting Midas was enough to fill even a hardened detective with trepidation, particularly when your boss had so recently put one of the gang leader's hard men in hospital. Not for nothing had Midas retained such a firm grip on his gang for the best part of twenty years. And what had Midas's lawyer meant when he said that his client was looking forward to meeting him? wondered Gallagher. He knew that Midas was perfectly capable of targeting police officers' families if he felt the need warranted such an action. Harris noticed his colleague's uneasy expression.

'Don't look so worried, Matty lad,' he said. 'It'll be alright, I promise you. Besides, if anyone does kick off when we see him, we can always put him in A & E as well, can't we?'

'Tell me why you were turned down for the Diplomatic Corps again?' said Gallagher gloomily.

Harris gave a low laugh and the remainder of the journey was spent in silence. The train pulled into Euston shortly after 1:00pm and the detectives immediately took a black cab to the publisher's office, where they presented themselves at the front desk. Miranda Hayes arrived in the foyer a couple of minutes later.

'Gentlemen, this is a surprise, we weren't expecting to see you again.' Her smile faded as she saw their grim expressions. 'Is something wrong?'

'We'd like to see Miss Murrell,' said Harris.

'I'm afraid that Miss Murrell is hosting a lunch for a group of national newspaper book reviewers in the boardroom. It's important that they are not disturbed so if you want to w–'

'Either you take us up or we'll go ourselves,' said Harris.

Hayes appeared for a moment as if she was about to remonstrate but one look at the inspector's stern expression was enough and, a couple of minutes later, the detectives were in the chief executive's office. They had just sat down when Murrell walked in, a thunderous look on her face.

'Would you care to explain what this is about?' she said angrily. 'I am not accustomed to being dragged–'

'James Cronin is dead,' said Harris.

The blood drained from the publisher's face and she sat down heavily behind her desk. It seemed to the detectives as if it was a genuine reaction.

'Dead?' she said. 'How?'

'He was shot,' said Harris. 'His body was found earlier this morning at a cottage in the Yorkshire Dales. Are you sure that you didn't know where he was, Miss Murrell?'

'None of us knew,' said Murrell. She glanced at her PA. 'Did we, Miranda?'

'He certainly didn't tell me,' said the PA. 'He said it was better that we did not know. I'm pretty sure that the same goes for the rest of the team.'

'Was there any sign of the book?' asked Murrell. 'A manuscript, the memory stick, maybe?'

'Two men are dead and all you can think about is the book?' exclaimed Gallagher.

'Yes, of course,' said Murrell hurriedly. 'I'm forgetting myself. It's a terrible tragedy, of course it is. However, I do have to be pragmatic.'

'Pragmatic?' snorted Gallagher. 'What does that mean?'

Murrell sighed.

'I'm not sure that you appreciate the importance of the book to the company, Sergeant,' she said. 'We took a gamble with David and agreed the biggest advance we have ever offered to a writer.'

'Why so much?' asked Harris.

'He was so adamant that he could deliver that we decided to make the book the centrepiece of our spring programme. It's the one that promises to take us to the next level. An international best-seller. I've started discussions about serialisations and a possible film deal and I've been priming the book reviewers sitting next door to expect something big.' She looked unhappily at the detectives. 'It'll be a disaster if it does not appear. Reputation is everything in this business and my board will be bound to ask questions. It could cost me my job.'

'At least you'll still be alive,' said Gallagher acerbically. 'Not a luxury that has been afforded to your writers. I hope it's worth it. Anyway, there was no sign of the book. Presumably, whoever killed James took it with him.'

Murrell buried her head in her hands.

'This is a nightmare,' she groaned.

The detectives watched her with little sympathy; they found her hard-headed approach difficult to take amid such tragic loss of life.

'Are you sure there isn't something you have been keeping from us?' asked Harris. 'These new angles that David had been chasing up, perhaps?'

'He wouldn't tell me what they were. He did promise that it was the final piece of the jigsaw, though. He said that it would make it the book of the year if he confirmed it.'

'Presumably James Cronin knew, though?' asked the inspector.

'All he said was there was someone he needed to interview then he would be able to let me have the finished manuscript and all would become clear.'

'But he didn't say who it was?'

'He said it would be better for him to confirm things first,' said Murrell.

Harris sighed, glanced at the wall clock and stood up.

'We'd better get going,' he said.

And the detectives left the publisher sitting silently in a room in which her dreams were crumbling fast.

# Chapter twenty

Gillian Roberts parked her car outside the Swaledale cottage just after 11:30am to be greeted at the gate by a tall, dark-haired man in his early fifties and wearing white overalls.

'DCI Geoff Smith,' he said. He extended a hand of welcome. 'You must be DI Roberts.'

'I am.'

'Good to meet you,' said Smith. 'Welcome to God's own country.'

'Don't let my governor hear you say that.'

'That would be Jack Harris, I take it?' said Smith as he led her up the path to the property.

'You know him?'

'Met him at a conference in Harrogate a couple of years ago. About bird of prey persecution, as I recall. Is he always a grumpy bastard?'

'He is, yes,' said Roberts with a smile. 'But a good copper.'

'I'm sure.' Smith pointed to a pile of white overalls lying on the ground outside the cottage. 'Suit up, please. Our forensics people are already in there.'

Smith watched her slip into the garment.

'You've just taken one of our people on,' he said as she finished dressing. 'Janet Maynard.'

'Yes, she's heading up our Special Branch.'

'How are you finding her?'

'I've not met her yet,' said Roberts. 'But, from what I've heard, she seems very efficient.'

'She's that, alright,' said Smith. He lowered his voice. 'If I may offer you a word of friendly advice, treat her with caution.'

'And why's that?'

'Plays it by the book, that one,' said Smith. 'Straight down the middle. No imagination. I went for that job and was amazed when they gave it to her. She'll not last long.'

'Duly noted,' said Roberts.

However, all the detective inspector had noted was yet another male senior officer bad-mouthing a successful woman and she'd heard it too many times before to be surprised. She followed Smith into the cottage and through to the kitchen. The body had been removed and one of the forensics officers was conducting a detailed examination of the scene.

'He was found there,' said Smith. He pointed to a pool of blood on the floor where Cronin had fallen.

'When was he killed?' asked Roberts. 'Do you know?'

'Our pathologist reckons it was sometime yesterday afternoon. Between one and six, she says, but she'll know more when she has conducted the PM later today.'

'Do we know how long Cronin had been living here?' asked Roberts.

'Just for a couple of days. It's a holiday let and he had leased it for three weeks. They're cheap out of season. You said on the phone that that there may be a link with the death of David Stabler?'

'You knew him?'

'He tried to get information out of me several times. I said no.'

'You did the right thing,' said Roberts.

'There's some as didn't. So what's the story?'

She outlined the circumstances surrounding the murder but stood by her promise to Harris not to mention Simon Jones. The instruction had preyed on her mind as she had driven up to Swaledale; it still felt wrong to withhold information from a fellow investigating officer and she hoped that they would be able to tell him soon enough.

'I take it you've still not found any evidence of the book?' she asked.

'Nope,' said Smith. 'Any idea what it was about?'

'All we know is that it's something to do with organised crime.' She tried to appear to be taking him in to her confidence. 'Between you and me, Geoff, Jack Harris and one of our detective sergeants are down in London at the moment, chasing something up. A gang leader by the name of Francis Jacques.'

'Midas?' said Smith.

'You know him, too?'

'Not personally – not sure I'd want to, from what I hear about him. However, there was a story on the front page of *The Daily News* a few weeks back about a detective superintendent who had been shagging a gang leader's wife. Not sure if you saw it?'

'We saw it,' said Roberts. 'It's what put us onto Midas.'

'Well, I attended police training college with the guy and, apparently, everyone knew that it was Midas's missus who had been doing the dirty with him.'

'It's a small world,' murmured Roberts.

'It is,' said Smith. He gave her a knowing look. 'Which is why it makes sense to share everything we know with each other, I would venture to suggest.'

'Of course,' said Roberts. She wondered if it was simply the sort of thing that Smith felt he had to say or whether or not he suspected that she knew more than she was letting on. His look suggested the latter; it was a troubling thought. Roberts decided to change the subject. 'I take it you've been doing door-to-door in the area?'

'We have, yes. Not that there's much to do. As you can see, it's a pretty remote location and we haven't turned up anything yet. Couple of unidentified vehicles, that's about it.'

'Neither of them from London, by any chance?'

'Scotland and Liverpool,' said Smith. 'Why do you ask?'

'It would seem that Midas sent a couple of his heavies to track down David Stabler a few weeks back. They nearly got him in Wakefield and they weren't far behind in Sheffield but the trail goes cold after that.'

'And you think that they might have got to Cronin?'

'We're not sure,' said Roberts. 'We'll know more after our guys meet Midas this afternoon.'

'So, how do you want to play it in the meantime?' asked Smith. 'Technically, James Cronin is our inquiry and my governor is keen that we keep it that way.'

'I am sure that we can work together.'

'I'm sure we can,' said Smith. He gave her another look. 'But I don't want to hear from the media that you have made an arrest. I want to know everything that's going on.'

'Of course,' said Roberts. 'We wouldn't dream of doing it any other way.'

# Chapter twenty-one

Harris and Gallagher arrived at the hotel ten minutes before the meeting with Francis Jacques was due to begin and were greeted in the foyer by the lawyer, a well-dressed man in his mid-thirties who smiled a welcome that appeared to be genuine. His handshake was firm and confident.

'Thank you for taking the time to come back to London so soon,' said Jeremy Rowley. 'We're on the second floor.'

A couple of minutes later, Rowley ushered the detectives into the room, which was dominated by a large oak table at the head of which sat a man with thinning brown hair streaked with wisps of grey and whose face was pock-marked with acne scars. Jacques may have been older than in the picture pinned on the noticeboard at Levton Bridge Police Station but he was instantly recognisable. The two men from the encounter with the detectives at the Indian restaurant stood along the side of the room. Lee Garritt's jaw was bruised and his lips were still swollen.

'Please take a seat, gentlemen,' said Jacques. He glanced at his minders. 'I assume you do not object to my associates being in attendance, Chief Inspector? I think that you will particularly remember Mr Garritt? He certainly remembers you.'

'I'm just trying to place him,' said Harris. His furrowed brow gave the appearance of someone trying to dredge up a long-buried memory as he and Gallagher sat down next to each other at the table. Eventually, the inspector gave a slight smile. 'Ah, yes, I have him now. Yes, happy for them to stay as long as they behave themselves.'

Garritt scowled but said nothing. For their part, the wary detectives were much more focused on Francis Jacques. A man whose reputation spread a long shadow across the capital, he looked unremarkable enough but something about his demeanour hinted at latent menace. Gallagher tried not to let his nerves show while Harris thought back to the gang leaders he had encountered over the years, particularly in his Greater Manchester Police days. He recognised at once the familiar glint in the eyes and knew that the calmness in Jacques's voice could not conceal the fact that he was dangerous and not to be under-estimated.

There was a knock on the door and a young hotel staff member entered bearing a loaded tray which she placed on the table.

'I took the liberty of ordering tea,' said Jacques. 'In my experience, police officers prefer it to coffee.'

The detectives nodded and the girl poured the drinks and hurriedly left the room. It seemed to Gallagher that she looked relieved to be out of there. He envied her.

'It's good to meet you at last, Chief Inspector,' said Jacques. He took a sip of tea then glanced at Garritt. 'Not many men can put Lee in hospital. I'm not surprised, though. Your reputation does precede you.'

'It does?'

'I did some checking with some of my associates in Manchester. They were glad to see the back of you when you left.'

'I'm sure they were,' said Harris. 'And I them.'

'And it's good to see Sergeant Gallagher as well,' said Jacques. He gave a slight smile as he surveyed the detective. 'Once one of Bermondsey's finest, I believe. You still have family there, I think? Your mother and one of your sisters.'

Gallagher nodded and resisted the temptation to demand how Jacques knew – the comment had done little to steady his nerves. Harris gave a thin smile. He had seen the tactic used several times during his time in Manchester but was not prepared to let it work here so he decided to steal the initiative. He had always found it to be the best way when dealing with powerful criminals.

'Why have you brought us all the way down here?' he said. 'We're very busy and can ill afford the time.'

His tone irked Jacques, whose eyes narrowed.

'You are here because certain stories are circulating about me in the media and I hold you responsible,' he said. 'I wish to set the record straight. I have had enough of these half-truths. They are very damaging.'

'So which half is true?' asked Harris. 'The bit about murdering David Stabler?'

Jacques angrily chewed his lip for a few moments while Gallagher held his breath. The sergeant had heard all the stories about Jacques, knew that men had been sent to the hospital for less. Or ended up in the morgue. Harris and Jacques glared at each other for a few moments. Jeremy Rowley took a seat at the table.

'Might I venture to suggest that calm heads are required here, gentlemen?' he said.

'Of course,' said Jacques. 'I apologise.'

Harris inclined his head slightly but said nothing.

'Before we start,' said Rowley, 'I would like to stress that this meeting is strictly off the record. Anything said in this room stays in this room. If it is repeated elsewhere, Mr Jacques will deny that the meeting ever occurred and will pursue action through the courts. Is that understood?'

Harris stood up.

'No conditions,' he said.

Jacques looked surprised but quickly recovered his composure and waved for him to sit down again.

'There's no need for any of that,' he said. 'I trust the chief inspector, Jeremy. I also trust that neither he nor his colleague are wearing wires.'

'You're welcome to check,' said Harris, who had remained standing.

Jacques shook his head.

'If my conversation with my colleagues in Manchester taught me anything,' he said, 'it is that you play the game straight.'

He glanced at Garritt and gave a slight smile.

'Besides,' he said. 'I have a strangely sentimental attachment to my teeth. Please, do sit. Have your cup of tea.'

Harris took his seat again and reached for his drink. Gallagher felt like he could breathe again.

'However,' said Jacques, his voice hardening, 'allow me to make my position absolutely clear. Idle gossip is one thing but it's different when my name is linked to serious crimes in media reports. I can take action against gossips but journalists are different.'

'But you did go after David Stabler, didn't you?' said Harris. 'You can't deny that and you must know how it looks.'

'I knew that he was writing a book and I believed it to be about me, yes.' Jacques glanced at his minders. 'And you are right, I did send a couple of my men to find him. The intention was to recover the manuscript, not to harm him. However, Mr Stabler evaded them.'

'So, they didn't kill him?' asked Harris. He gave the minders a hard look.

'They did not,' said Jacques. His voice remained calm. 'The encounter in Wakefield was the last time they saw him and by the time they tracked him down to Sheffield he was long gone. My men returned to London after that and the next I heard was that he had been murdered.'

'And can we assume that it was your men who assaulted the nightwatchman at the publishers?' asked Gallagher. It was the first time he had spoken since entering the room and he found himself overwhelmed by a feeling that he needed to assert himself.

'That was unfortunate,' said Jacques. He glanced at Garritt, who looked down at his feet. 'I do so hate unnecessary unpleasantness. There was no intention to harm him.'

'And what about James Cronin?' asked Harris. 'Presumably, you were looking for him as well?'

'Cronin?' asked Jacques. 'I have not heard of him.'

'Come on, if you knew that David Stabler was writing a book, it's safe to assume that you know he asked James Cronin to complete the work if anything happened to him.'

'I know nothing about that,' repeated Jacques. 'I did not know that anyone else was working on the book. We have certainly had no interaction with him.'

'Interaction!' exclaimed Gallagher. 'The man's dead, for God sake!'

A mixture of surprise and consternation flickered across Jacques's face. To the detectives, the reaction appeared genuine.

'Dead?' he said.

'His body was found this morning in a cottage in the Yorkshire Dales,' said Harris. 'Someone shot him.'

Jacques considered the comment for a few moments.

'And the book?' he asked. 'Do you know where it is?'

'It's still missing,' said Gallagher. 'Presumably whoever committed the murders has it.'

Midas pursed his lips.

'That is a pity,' he said. 'I hate to think what it says about me.'

'Well, I can put your mind at rest on that score,' said Harris. 'According to the publisher, it's not about you.'

'Really?' Again, Jacques's surprise seemed genuine. 'Then what was it about?'

'I can't tell you that. Suffice to say, we are pursuing several lines of inquiry.'

'And am I still one of them?'

'I suspect not,' said Harris. 'And for what it's worth, any suggestion in the media that we were interested in you did not come from me or any of my team.'

'Our conversation would seem to be at an end then,' said Jacques. He stood up. 'Perhaps you could be so kind as to inform the media of the fact, if the opportunity arises? I've got enough problems with things that I have done without having to worry about things that I haven't. I'm sure you understand.'

'I understand,' said Harris.

'Have a safe journey home,' said Jacques, heading for the door. 'I trust we will not have cause to meet again. Good day, gentlemen.'

And with that he was gone. Lee Garritt paused at the door to give the inspector a dirty look. Harris smiled affably.

'Goodbye, Lee,' he said. 'Missing you already.'

Garritt scowled and followed Jacques and his entourage into the corridor.

'Come on,' said Harris when they had gone. 'Let's get out of here.'

'You'll get no argument from me there,' said Gallagher.

Once the detectives were out of the building, they began to walk down the busy street towards the cafe where they had agreed to meet Danny Mahler before taking the train back north. Gallagher was silent.

'I sense that something is bugging you,' said Harris.

'Do you not think that we let him off lightly? I mean, the man's totally untrustworthy.'

'He may well be, Matty lad, but his surprise when we told him about Cronin seemed genuine. No, I believe him.'

'And then there was one,' said Gallagher. 'Our killer has got to be Simon Jones.'

Harris did not reply.

'I know that look,' said Gallagher. 'The cogs are whirring in that brain of yours. You reckon that we should be looking at someone else?'

Harris shrugged.

'The honest truth?' he said. 'I do not know for certain.'

'But you suspect someone?'

Before Harris could reply, his mobile phone rang. It was Graham Leckie.

'Graham,' he said. 'What can I do for you?'

'You still interested in this Simon Jones fellow?' asked the Greater Manchester Police intelligence officer.

'Yeah, we are. Why, you got something on him?'

'Only someone who remembers him from Dusseldorf in the mid-eighties.' Leckie sounded proud of himself. 'An ex-cop. Would you like to meet him?'

'Sure would,' said Harris. 'But I'm in London with Matty then in a meeting first thing tomorrow morning. Can we fix it for the afternoon, do you think?'

'Any chance you can break your journey back tonight?' asked Leckie.

'Is what he has to say that good?'

'I don't know but he's flying out from Manchester Airport to visit his daughter in South Africa early tomorrow morning and he won't be back for seven weeks.'

'OK, we'll stop off at Manchester Piccadilly on our way back,' said Harris. 'But I'd like to meet at one of the coffee shops at the station rather than go into the city, if possible. Word does seem to get round rather fast whenever I go back to Manchester and I've had enough of goons for one day.'

'Fair enough. Text me when you're due to get in and I'll sort something out. I hope it turns out to be worth the trouble.'

Harris ended the call but his phone rang again immediately.

'What it is to be loved,' he said.

'DCI Harris,' said a woman's voice. 'It's Control Room. We've just had a call from a Professor Neal Radcliffe at Roxham General Hospital. He's asked you to ring him. Says he's got some information for you.'

## Chapter twenty-two

The detectives settled themselves at a corner table in a cafe round the corner from Euston Station, placed their order with the waitress and Harris called Roxham General Hospital.

'Can you put me through to Professor Radcliffe, please?' he said when the switchboard answered. 'Professor Radcliffe? Jack Harris. You wanted to speak to me.'

'I did,' said the psychiatrist. 'I said that I would show the letter you left with me to colleagues. I'm sorry it's taken a while to get back to you but, like I said, these are busy people.'

'I appreciate them giving up their time to look at it,' said Harris. 'But we've come round to the way of thinking that it's a fake.'

'Then I would think again,' said Radcliffe. 'I sent copies to four people, all eminent experts in the field. Although one of them was not prepared to commit himself, the others were of the opinion that it could well be genuine.'

'Really?'

'Of course, they would have to meet him to be sure but their belief is that the idea should not be discounted.'

'So, you're saying that whoever wrote it really is suffering from some form of dementia?'

Gallagher looked at the inspector and raised an eyebrow.

'Very possibly, yes,' said Radcliffe. 'The crumbling mind is capable of believing just about anything. One of my elderly patients thought he was an Egyptian pharaoh. A somewhat grandiose delusion for someone who stacked shelves at Tesco, might I suggest.'

'But what about the fact that he created all these fake identities?' asked Harris. 'Surely, a crumbling mind would not be capable of actions that sophisticated?'

'Who says they're fake?' said Radcliffe. 'He may well believe them to be real. In my experience, dementia patients can become quite aggressive if you try to persuade them otherwise. Besides, as I mentioned last time we met, people with dementia have periods of clarity when, to all intents and purposes, there is nothing wrong with them. Sometimes, they can be quite sustained periods of time.'

'And how long would it be before someone gets really bad?'

'It varies,' said the professor. 'Some conditions can be very gradual but some can develop in steps. A person can go to bed with mild symptoms and wake up the next morning significantly worse. It's not an exact science but we already knew that the mental health of someone living in isolation, as was the case with your man, could deteriorate rapidly. The pandemic reminded us of that fact.'

'I see.' Harris nodded his thanks as the waitress approached the table with their drinks and sandwiches. 'And in your opinion, could a man like that be capable of murder?'

'There have certainly been cases of people with dementia committing such crimes,' said Radcliffe. 'Although I have to say that they tended to be more impulsive than the scenario we are talking about here. I gave evidence at the trial of an old man in a care home who struck his wife with a vase. However, having read the media reports, this case sounds like it has far too much organisation about it so, on the balance of probabilities, I would say no.'

Harris thanked him and ended the call.

'I got the gist of that,' said Gallagher. 'And then there were none. Looks like we're out of suspects.'

Harris did not reply but took a sip of tea instead. At that moment, Danny Mahler entered the cafe. Gallagher waved a hand and the Metropolitan Police officer came over and sat down at the table. Gallagher slid a sandwich over towards him and pointed to the empty third cup.

'Cheers,' said Mahler. He glanced round at the cafe, which was half-full. 'I don't see any of Midas's men, thank goodness.'

'We've just been with them,' said Harris. He took a sip of his tea. 'Lee Garritt did not exactly look pleased to see us, did he, Matty lad?'

'Distinctly unimpressed, I'd say.'

'Yeah, well, he's been bad-mouthing you to anyone who will listen,' said Mahler. 'I say bad-mouthing but he's not capable of much in the way of speech at the moment. I think he's more embarrassed than angry. He's lost face, thanks to you. How'd it go with Midas, anyway?'

'Very civilized,' said Harris. He glanced at Gallagher. 'Apart from the odd veiled threat. We had a nice cup of tea together. Best china cups.'

'Yeah, that's how he operates,' said Mahler. 'Nice as pie then sends someone round to rearrange your kneecaps. Do you still fancy him for your murders?'

'Not really,' said Harris.

'Where does that leave you then?'

'Square one,' said Gallagher.

'Sorry,' said Mahler.

An hour later, the two Levton Bridge detectives were sitting in the train as it pulled out of Euston Station and began the long journey northward. Looking out of the window, Gallagher noticed Lee Garritt standing at the far end of the platform. As the train pulled alongside, Garritt caught Gallagher's eye, made the shape of a gun with his fingers, gave a slight smile and pretended to pull the trigger. Gallagher frowned as his thoughts turned to his mother and the other members of his family in London. Harris read his mind.

'They'll be alright,' said the inspector. 'He knows that I'll knock the rest of his teeth out if he tries anything.'

'But you'll run out of teeth, one day. What happens then?'

Harris did not reply and Gallagher went back to staring out of the window.

* * *

Alison Butterfield was the only officer in the CID squad room when one of the desk phones rang.

'You able to come down to reception?' asked a voice. 'We've got someone here who reckons he might have some useful information about the murder up at Haggs Scarr.'

'Sure.'

Butterfield grinned and left the room. She had spent much of her time in recent days feeling increasingly sidelined, engaged in desk-bound research while others were out and about, and the thought of being involved in something more proactive filled her with anticipation. Filled with an intense desire to prove herself to her superiors, particularly given all the praise Sally Orr had been receiving, she bounded down the stairs. A couple of minutes later, she was sitting in the interview room off reception with a young man who was wearing the livery of a well-known delivery company. He seemed nervous.

'So, what do you want to tell me, Mr Ross?' asked Butterfield.

'I hope I'm not wasting your time.' Mally Ross frowned. 'But this has been nagging away at me for a few days. It's something that happened the day the radio said that fellow was shot dead. I keep thinking it might be important.'

'How come it took you so long to come in?'

'It's the first time I've been back in Levton Bridge since it happened. There's another reason, though. I'm not supposed to pick up hitch-hikers and I'll get the sack if my bosses find out.'

'We'll try and avoid that happening, if we can,' said Butterfield. She tried not to let her excitement show, to present herself as matter-of-fact and professional in the face of what was potentially a first sighting of the murderer following the shooting. 'Why don't you start at the beginning?'

'I deliver to the vets in Levton Bridge a couple of times a week,' said Ross. 'I was heading into town on the road from Carperwith when I saw him.'

'Saw who exactly?'

'This old feller walking along the road.'

'Where?' asked Butterfield.

'A couple of miles past one of the cottages – Hillview, it's called.'

As Butterfield made a note on her pad, she could feel her pulse racing – this was a breakthrough and it had fallen into the young detective's lap.

'Are you sure it was Hillview?' she asked. She tried to sound as if she was not that interested.

'Yeah. I've been driving that route for two years. Go past the sign every week. Never seen the old chap before, mind.'

The constable reached into her jacket pocket and produced a photocopy of the German police photograph of Simon Jones.

'Is that him?' she asked.

Ross examined the image for a few moments.

'He was much older,' he said eventually.

'It's a very old picture,' said Butterfield.

'I suppose it *could* be him.'

'Anyway, you picked him up?' said Butterfield. 'Why did you do that if you're not allowed?'

'There was something about him. It wouldn't have felt right leaving him there. He looked like he needed help. He came over as kinda lost and it was raining hard. It was the day we had that big storm.'

'What did he look like?'

'Late sixties, early seventies, maybe. Grey hair.'

Butterfield's eyes gleamed.

'Did he say where he was going?' she asked.

'Preston.'

'Why Preston? Did he say?'

'He didn't say much, really,' said Ross. 'He seemed kind of distracted. Kept muttering to himself. I wondered whether to bring him here, actually, in case he'd got out of a home or something – he only had a small bag with him – but when we stopped in the marketplace and saw the bus stop, he perked up. Said he'd catch the bus.'

'So, you left him there?'

'I was going to but the weather was so crap and the bus shelter is not covered so I offered to take him as far as Carlisle – I had a couple of deliveries in the area. Last I saw of him was when I dropped him off at the bus station.'

'Can you remember exactly what time that was?' asked Butterfield.

'I can.' Ross produced a piece of paper from his jacket pocket and slid it across the desk towards her. He gave her a rueful look. 'This is my time sheet. We live by the clock.'

Butterfield scanned the document.

'Tight schedule,' she said.

'Yeah. My drop-off in Levton Bridge was due at 12:15 so I'd have picked him up a quarter of an hour or so before then. My last drop-off in Carlisle was just past three, I think it says.'

Butterfield ran her hand down the sheet and nodded.

'Eleven minutes past,' she said. 'Can I keep this?'

'Be my guest.'

'Anything else you want to mention?'

'Like what?' asked Ross.

'I dunno.' Butterfield realised that she would finally have to show her hand. 'Did he have blood on him, maybe?'

'Na, nothing like that. Why, do you think he was the one who's killed that bloke in the tent?'

'Just thought I'd check,' said Butterfield. She stood up. 'Thank you for your help, Mr Ross. You've been very helpful. Very helpful, indeed.'

'So, who was he?' asked the delivery driver.

'The last man alive,' said Butterfield. 'That's who he was.'

After seeing him out of the police station, the detective constable rushed off to find Roberts, who had returned from North Yorkshire and was in her office catching up on reports from the team.

'Interesting,' said Roberts when the constable had recounted the details of the conversation. 'It would seem to turn our attention back to the dementia theory. It also explains why he appeared to have vanished into thin air. Like Jack Harris says, there's always a rational explanation for these things.'

'So, what do we do now?'

'Well, for starters, I want you to get hold of the bus companies that use Carlisle bus station,' said the detective inspector. 'See if they've got any CCTV that might help us.'

'It'll be like looking for a needle in a haystack.'

'Maybe not if we circulate his description to other forces. And I'll get in touch with an old pal of mine. She's a chief inspector in Preston. It's a long shot, I know, but maybe we'll get lucky.'

'Do you think it was him?' asked Butterfield. 'Do you think it was Simon Jones?'

'I do,' said Roberts. 'And at last we're on his trail.'

## Chapter twenty-three

Harris and Gallagher left the northbound train as agreed and were soon sitting in one of the cafes at Manchester Piccadilly Railway Station, opposite a slim dark-haired man and a distinguished-looking grey-haired pensioner.

'Can I introduce you to Michael Fischer?' said Graham Leckie, the younger of the two. 'Michael, meet DCI Harris and DS Gallagher.'

Fischer shook their hands.

'Good to meet you, gentlemen,' he said. His voice had only the slightest hint of a German accent. 'I'm not sure how much I can help you, though. It was all a long time ago.'

'Anything you can tell us would be useful,' said Harris. 'Simon Jones is still a bit of a mystery.'

'He always was,' said Fisher. 'Very secretive.'

'I found Michael by asking round some contacts in Manchester,' explained Leckie. 'He was a detective with the West German police in the mid-eighties. He came over here in 1989. That's right, isn't it, Michael?'

'I married an English girl,' said Fischer. 'Left the police and worked for a security company. Graham tells me that you are trying to work out if Simon Jones was involved in your murders?'

'We are,' said Harris.

'I have to say that I was surprised when he rang me about him. I haven't heard the name in years. I didn't know Jones personally but I did have contacts in the Dusseldorf area and you do hear things.'

'Like what?' asked Harris.

Fischer glanced round before continuing with lowered voice.

'What you have to understand,' he said, 'is that, in his heyday, Simon Jones was big league, as was the gang. He was the one who planned the jobs.'

'So, he was perfectly capable of planning the break-out from the prison van?' asked Gallagher.

'It was his kind of scheme. He always had a flair for the dramatic, did Simon.' Fischer frowned. 'There was something not quite right about it.'

'In what way?' asked Harris.

Fischer hesitated and glanced at Leckie.

'You can trust them,' said the Greater Manchester officer.

'I would certainly appreciate it if it didn't go any further,' said Fischer. 'I am still bound by certain restrictions, as I am sure you can understand. What I can say is that there was talk at the time of the break-out that someone had passed information on to the men who attacked the van. They knew exactly which route the vehicle was taking and when it would be there. That kind of information could have only come from someone on the inside.'

'Any idea who would do that?' asked Gallagher.

'It was all gossip and nothing was ever proved but the assumption was that it was someone in the prison service. I'm pretty sure that it wasn't anyone from the police.'

'Why not?' asked Harris.

'The team that investigated the gang was led by a senior detective called Schulz. His second in command was a bloke called Neumann. I knew them both pretty well and would have said that they were straight up. Same for their team. They'd been after the gang for the best part of a year and I'm sure that they would not have done anything to jeopardise the inquiry.'

'We may need to talk to them, anyway,' said Harris.

'You'll struggle. Ernest Schulz passed away from cancer six years ago and Walter Neumann died of a heart attack last year.'

'What about the other members of the gang?' asked Harris. 'Any of them still around?'

'Some of the younger ones lower down the hierarchy might be, I suppose, but not the ringleaders. One of them died in a fight in prison, another had a stroke in his cell and the third one was killed in a car accident a few weeks after getting out.'

'Leaving Simon Jones as the last man alive,' said Harris. He glanced at Gallagher. 'The only one of the main players who could tell the story to Stabler.'

'Ah, yes, Graham mentioned a book,' said Fischer.

'We are working on the theory that the last thing Jones wanted was his whereabouts to be revealed, particularly not by a journalist,' said Gallagher.

'That makes sense,' said Fischer. 'There's plenty of people who would like to speak to him, I am sure. He certainly went out of his way to disappear. I'm in touch with a few friends from the old days and they tell me that he was never seen again. The word was that he had managed to hide away enough money to live out the rest of his days in peaceful anonymity.'

'Apparently not,' said Harris. 'Apparently, he's still active and involved with terrorists.'

Fischer looked surprised.

'Who told you that?' he said.

'The German police.'

'Well, they would know, I suppose, although I'd struggle to believe it. I know that I've been out of things for a long time but nothing I am hearing from my pals suggests that Simon Jones is still active. If he is, it must be a new gang. The old one never got back together, that's for sure.'

Harris was silent for a few moments as the idea that had been developing in the back of his mind for a couple of days started to force its way to the forefront. An idea that he had not wanted to consider. An idea that he never wanted to consider whenever it raised its ugly head. The inspector looked at Gallagher, whose eyes betrayed how troubled he was at thinking the same thing. The sergeant opened his mouth to speak but Harris silenced him with a look.

'Are you absolutely sure about this?' asked Harris, returning his attention to Fischer. 'That he's not active?'

'That's certainly what I heard. However, you'll appreciate that I haven't worked for the police for years so I only pick up the odd bit of gossip and most of that is probably way out of date. You'd have to ask one of the current detectives for the more up-to-date stuff.'

'Maybe we will,' said Harris.

'But I will say one thing,' said Fischer. 'From what I've heard about Simon Jones, he is not the kind of man to commit violent acts. He was horrified when those people were hurt in the gang's robberies and he'd have felt the same when the prison guard was shot dead. Murder was just not his style.'

Harris thought of the photograph pinned up on the noticeboard at Levton Bridge Police Station. Thought of the amused glint in the eyes.

'No,' murmured Harris. 'No, I suspect it isn't.'

The Levton Bridge detectives left the cafe just as the next northbound train was due to depart and it was only when they had taken their seats that Gallagher spoke.

'Why would German police say…?' he began.

'It's a good question,' said Harris. He sighed. 'And I have this awful feeling that we both know the answer but we're trying not to think it.'

'I suspect you're right,' said Gallagher.

# Chapter twenty-four

The next morning, having again walked the dogs across the hills in the half-light of pre-dawn, Jack Harris loaded them into the Land Rover and headed for his 9:00am meeting at force headquarters. Joining the inspector and Janet Maynard in the head of Special Branch's office was Charlie Bourne and a tall, dark-haired man with a neatly-trimmed moustache, smartly dressed in a black shirt and jeans. He stood up as the inspector entered the room and extended a hand in welcome.

'Josef Haller,' he said. 'Although I would very much appreciate it if my name is not mentioned outside this office. I undertake extensive undercover work and do everything I can to protect my identity.'

'Of course,' said Harris.

The inspector shook his hand, sat down and studied the Dusseldorf police officer with interest for a few moments, rapidly concluding that he was the kind of man who expected to get his own way. The inspector resolved to give Haller the impression that he would be able to achieve just that. Harris had already decided to keep his suspicions to himself; the ugly thought from the previous evening had continued to develop and he didn't like it.

Haller, for his part, seemed determined to show due deference to the inspector.

'I am sorry to have caused you so much trouble,' he said. 'I find this situation truly regrettable. I know that you are only doing your job and I would have felt similarly frustrated if the positions were reversed.'

'Thank you,' said Harris. 'And I realise that you're only doing your job as well. Given that, I am sure that we can find a way of working together that allows both of us to achieve our aims.'

Haller inclined his head slightly.

'So, what *is* the solution?' said Janet Maynard. She was relieved at the reasonable approach of both men. The last thing she needed was a full-blown diplomatic incident just weeks into the job. 'After all, we are both after Simon Jones, are we not?'

'We are,' said Haller. 'Although, I do have to emphasise that our view has not changed on the matter. We still regard ourselves as having priority on him.'

'If he's so important, how come you've not tracked him down when you've had the best part of forty years to do it?'

Haller gave the inspector a rueful look.

'I believe the English phrase is a "standing joke",' he said.

'What does that mean?' asked Harris.

'The task has been passed from officer to officer down the generations,' said Haller. 'But I'm not sure that they have tried very hard to find him, particularly as the years have passed. Simon Jones had been regarded very much as ancient history and what few records we have on him are largely incomplete. No one even knew if he was still alive.'

'So what changed?'

'Suddenly, he became of great interest. When my predecessor retired last year, the Simon Jones file landed on my desk but I'll be honest with you, I had not planned to expend much effort on it, either. Then the rumours began to circulate that he was still an active criminal who had connections with terrorism. The problem was that we had no idea where he was.'

'Until we triggered the alert in the fingerprints database,' said Harris.

'That's right. Since it was a low-key operation, I could not risk circulating his details so I put the alert there to see if anyone stumbled across him. I didn't think anyone would after all this time – I thought he was dead – and I couldn't believe my luck when your Mr Guthrie tried to access the fingerprint record. To find out where Simon Jones was after all this time was truly remarkable.'

'Except we lost him again.'

'Yes, that was unfortunate,' said Haller. 'Do you have any idea where he went?'

'We are pretty sure that he's no longer in our area. I've got officers carrying out checks but I'm not particularly hopeful of tracking him down. The man has shown great skill to stay hidden for the best part of forty years and we have no idea where he went.'

Haller gave a frustrated suck of the teeth.

'That is a pity,' he said. 'We were rather hoping that with the passage of time, he might be minded to co-operate with us.'

'But, surely, he's in his seventies?' said Harris. 'Can he really know anything of use?'

'We believe that he remains a formidable strategist. He is exceptionally creative and he retains his criminal connections.'

'But how do you plan to persuade him to work with you even if you do find him?' asked Harris. 'He's not exactly shown much inclination to work with the police in the past, has he?'

'You forget that there is still an outstanding warrant for his arrest. He's got a prison sentence hanging over him, not to mention some difficult questions to answer about the death of the prison guard. We hope that he may agree to assist us with our inquiries in return for making it all go away and offering him protection.'

'Which would mean, of course, that I could not charge him with murder,' said Harris.

'I am afraid it would, yes. But, from what I hear, your evidence against him is somewhat thin anyway. Something about a book but no one has even seen the manuscript? Besides, from what Charlie tells me about this Stabler fellow, he had many enemies. Forgive me, Chief Inspector, but it does rather sound like you are grasping at straws.'

Harris gave Bourne a sharp look but said nothing.

'Anyway, the book is of little interest to us,' continued Haller. 'Our operation will have been completed long before it is published – *if* it is published. The people in whom we are interested are planning a series of atrocities across Europe in the next few weeks and, I'm sorry, Chief Inspector, but that's more important than your inquiry. Two deaths against the potential for many.'

'I would beg to differ.'

'I think we both know who your chief constable would back if it came to it. He is unlikely to want his force to be embroiled in a dispute between governments.' Haller looked at Maynard. 'Don't you agree, Janet?'

Maynard gave Harris an apologetic look.

'Sorry, Jack,' she said. 'I've already asked the question on the top floor and my hands are tied on this one. Yours, too, might I suggest. This is just too big.'

'I do not seem to have much in the way of options,' said Harris through pursed lips. 'You asked about a solution, Janet, well, it would appear to be me doing as I'm told. This seems to be a game played by Josef's rules.'

Haller gave a slight smile.

'Some you win, Chief Inspector,' he said. 'I would suggest that you stop actively pursuing Jones but let me know if you do hear anything interesting and we can take it from there. I am sure that your Special Branch can assist us in returning him to Germany if he does turn up.'

Janet Maynard nodded.

'Of course,' she said.

'In which case,' said Haller, standing up, 'I thank you for your time. If I'm quick, I might just make the mid-afternoon flight back.'

* * *

Half an hour later, a deeply troubled Harris was driving back to Levton Bridge when his mobile phone rang. Number withheld. He took the call.

'It's DCI Geoff Smith, over at North Yorkshire,' said a voice. 'I thought you'd like an update on our investigation into the death of James Cronin.'

'I certainly would, Geoff. You got anything?'

'A possible sighting of the killer. A man was seen walking down the road towards the cottage about an hour before we think that Cronin was shot. He was spotted by a local shepherd.'

'Description?'

'Not much, I am afraid,' said Smith. 'Tall. Slim. His face was largely covered by a hood.'

'Age?'

'The shepherd reckons thirties, forties, but he could not be sure. Any of this tie in what you've come up with?'

Harris thought for a few moments then made up his mind. Time to take back control of the game.

'We'd been looking at someone older,' he said. 'Much older.'

'This Midas character?'

'No, someone else.'

'Your DI never mentioned another suspect when she came over here.' Smith did not attempt to conceal his irritation. 'I went out of my way to co-operate fully with her and now I find that the bloody woman has been holding out on me.'

'I'd thank you to show more respect for Gillian,' said Harris. 'Besides, she was under orders from me not to tell you.'

'Why on earth would you do that?'

'There's something we haven't been able to share before now. Somewhat of a complication. Special Branch are involved.'

'That'll be the delightful Ms Maynard, will it?' said Smith. He gave a snort of derision. 'I told your DI that she couldn't be trusted. Too straight-laced, that one.'

'What did I say about respect?'

Smith was about to utter a retort but the edge to the inspector's voice made him think better of the idea; he sensed that the time had come for diplomacy, if only for the sake of his investigation.

'I'm sorry,' he said. 'I'm just annoyed. I mean, why are Special Branch interfering in a straightforward murder investigation?'

'Because it's not straightforward and they've been backed into a corner. We all have.'

'Including you?'

'Not anymore,' said Harris.

## Chapter twenty-five

Jack Harris walked into the CID squad room at Levton Bridge Police Station, where half a dozen officers were at work.

'How'd it go with our German friend?' said Roberts, breaking off from a conversation with Butterfield.

'Not good,' said Harris. He sat down at one of the desks. 'If what we were told about Simon Jones last night is correct, our Mr Haller has just spent forty-five minutes lying his head off to me. Trouble is, I'm not sure why. One thing's certain, he's got Special Branch and the chief constable eating out of his hand and...'

The inspector's voice tailed off as he noticed that Sally Orr had started to leaf rapidly through a pile of print-outs lying on her desk. The constable noticed that everyone was watching her.

'You got something?' asked Harris.

'It may be nothing,' said the constable. 'But did you say the German officer you've just met is called Haller?'

Harris nodded.

'Yeah,' he said. 'Josef Haller. He's an intelligence officer with the police in Dusseldorf. Why?'

'Because it's not the first time I have seen that name,' said Orr. She located the print-out she was searching for and held up a copy of a newspaper article for him to see. 'Our friendly librarian emailed another batch of stuff late yesterday. One of the documents is a report on what appears to have been an inquest into the murder of the guard during the prison van break-out.'

'And?' asked Harris. He leaned forward in his chair.

'Well, it may be a coincidence, but three police officers gave evidence.' Orr scanned through the document. 'A guy called Schulz, one called Neumann and a man called Thomas Haller.'

Harris looked round the room at the other officers.

'Josef's father?' he said.

'It's not beyond the bounds of possibility,' said Gallagher.

Harris returned his attention to Orr.

'I don't believe in coincidences, particularly when it comes to murder inquiries,' he said. 'Schulz and Neumann ran the operation to arrest the gang but we didn't know about Thomas Haller. What was his involvement, Sally?'

Orr ran her finger down the document.

'He seems to have been a more junior member of the investigation team,' she said. 'He told the hearing that police believed that Simon Jones had left the country.'

Harris slapped his hand onto the desk in triumph.

'I told you we were missing something.' He looked at Roberts. 'I reckon it's high time we made that phone call to Germany. You're right, we shouldn't have left it this long. And we need to find Simon Jones before the Germans. If I'm right, he could well be the next intended victim.'

'Not the killer?' asked Roberts.

'I suspect not,' replied Harris. 'See, I have this awful feeling that Josef Haller has been playing us for fools.'

Roberts's mobile phone rang. She listened for a couple of minutes then ended the call and looked at Harris.

'It looks like we won't have to wait long,' she said. 'That was my pal at Preston police. They think that they might have found Simon Jones.'

'Excellent,' said Harris. He headed for the door and motioned for Gallagher to follow him. 'Perhaps he can shed some light on what the hell has been happening.'

'I shouldn't get your hopes up,' said Roberts.

Harris gave her a quizzical look.

'You'll see,' she said.

Having reluctantly left the dogs with the secretary again, Harris guided the Land Rover towards the southbound M6 and, two and a half hours later, he brought the vehicle to a halt next to the patrol car parked outside an ivy-covered nursing home on the edge of Preston. Harris and Gallagher got out of the vehicle to be met at the front door by a fresh-faced young uniformed officer.

'Hello, sir,' he said. 'Constable Barry Gordon. My chief inspector suggested that I come to meet you. I work the area around the bus station. That's where your man was found.'

'Before we see him, it might be helpful if you go through the whole story again,' said Harris. 'Just so that we're clear in our mind.'

'Sure, they have a nice cafe here. Fancy a cuppa?'

'Always,' said Harris.

A few minutes later, the three officers were sitting at a table in the pleasant, airy cafe, its walls adorned with large paintings of flowers to give the room a cheerful feel. Cups of tea and fruit scones sat on the table.

'I hope I'm not wasting your time, sir,' said Gordon. He took a sip of his tea. 'The description on the note my chief inspector circulated could be anyone with grey hair, really, but something about it rang a bell and if there's even the slightest chance…'

Harris nodded approvingly.

'It's smart work, whether it's him or not,' he said. 'You picked him up the morning after he took the bus from Carlisle, I think?'

'We did, yes.' Gordon took a bite of scone and chewed for a few moments before continuing. 'We've run through the bus station CCTV and saw him getting off a bus from Carlisle the previous evening. The staff reported him to us the next morning because he'd spent the night there and was wandering around looking confused. Easily done. Preston bus station is a confusing place at the best of times even if you've got all your marbles.'

'It is indeed,' said Harris.

'You know it?'

'I do.' Harris nodded. He recalled the arrest of a major gang member there when he was with Greater Manchester Police and had headed up a joint operation with the Lancashire constabulary. 'Did Simon Jones try to get away when you approached him?'

'No, he was good as gold, but he calls himself George Garvie, although we can't prove that's his name. He was not carrying any ID. He seemed quite relieved to see us, actually. Did not seem to know where he was. He said he was surprised to see so many people. I didn't understand that.'

'He thinks he's the last man alive,' said Gallagher. 'Dementia.'

'We'd guessed that it was something like that. That's why he's in this place.' Gordon shook his head. 'We get so many of these mental health cases these days. Anyway, we took him to see one of the force's doctors, just to be sure.'

'And did the doctor confirm it?' asked Gallagher.

'She did, yes. Alzheimer's, probably.' Gordon gestured to the cafe with a waft of the hand. 'She referred him here. The council's picking up the tab until they work out what to do with him.'

'I take it there was no sign of violence on him when you picked him up?' asked Harris. 'No blood or bruises?'

‘No, nothing like that. That’s why I was surprised to discover that you wanted him for murder.’ Gordon reached into his tunic pocket and produced a document, which he handed to Harris. ‘I thought you might like to see the doctor’s official report. I got her to print out a copy for you.’

‘Good lad.’

Gordon gave the inspector time to scan the document and pass it to Gallagher.

‘Do you still think he killed those journalists?’ asked the constable once the inspector had finished reading.

Harris studied him intently for a few moments, alerted by an uncertainty in his voice.

‘Well, we had wondered if he was faking dementia,’ he said.

Gordon hesitated, wondering if he had gone too far in questioning such a senior officer’s judgement. Harris guessed what he was thinking.

‘I don’t bite,’ he said.

Gallagher thought of Lee Garritt’s missing teeth.

‘And neither do those he falls out with,’ he said.

Gordon looked confused. Jack Harris gave a slight smile.

‘Just tell me what you’re thinking,’ he said.

‘Well, I’m no expert, sir, but I’m not sure that he is faking dementia.’ Gordon nodded towards the doctor’s report. ‘And neither does she. Besides, I don’t think that the man that we picked up could have done anything like that, even if he was in his right mind. He seems a gentle sort of soul, really.’

## Chapter twenty-six

The detectives finished their snacks as Gordon went to summon a member of staff, who led them along a corridor and into a side room, where Simon Jones was sitting, staring out of the window into a small courtyard populated with fruit trees and shrubs. Birds crowded round a couple of feeders hanging from a washing line. The detectives looked at Jones with interest, viewing him despite their better judgement in the way they would if confronted by a celebrity about whom they had heard so much. A slim man with greying, thinning hair, his demeanour confirmed what they had come to believe with growing conviction, that the Simon Jones of the stories had gone to be replaced by a man not of this world but rather one beset by confusion and bewilderment. Gallagher recalled similar thoughts from his father's final days and found himself battling to control his emotions.

'You OK?' said Harris quietly.

Gallagher nodded but did not speak. He was not sure he would have been capable of words in that moment.

'Mr Garvie,' said the nurse. She reached down to tap Simon Jones gently on the arm. 'There's some people here to see you. They are police officers and they wish to ask you some questions.'

The old man turned blank eyes on them. The nurse looked at the detectives.

'Don't be too long,' she said. 'He's not really sure who or where he is, I am afraid. I'm not sure he's capable of telling you anything and I'm not sure I'd believe it, anyway.'

The detectives nodded and sat down on the bed. Gordon remained by the door, leaning against the wall and relishing his involvement in the investigation. He had long since harboured ambitions of transferring to CID.

'Mr Jones?' said Harris. 'Or may I call you Simon?'

It seemed to the inspector that there was a brief flicker of recognition from Jones but it was momentary and had gone within seconds. He did not look at the new arrivals but continued to stare out of the window.

'We would like to ask you some questions about what happened at Hillview Cottage,' said Harris.

'I don't know about no cottage,' said Jones. It was the first time he had spoken since the police officers had entered the room and his voice was quiet and flat. Finally, he turned to look at the inspector. 'I have been in China all this year. You should know that.'

Harris glanced at the nurse and raised an eyebrow.

'China?' he asked.

'He keeps saying he's been there on business,' she explained. 'He says that it was something to do with advertising. I don't know if he maybe did that as a job? Like a lot of dementia cases, he does have moments of clarity before he slips back again but it's difficult to work out what's true and what's in his imagination.'

Gallagher nodded.

'My dad was like that,' he said. 'Thought he was a ship's captain, at one stage. The only ship he'd ever captained was when he took us to the boating lake at the park one Sunday and, even then, he ran it aground.'

Harris gave his sergeant a slight smile then turned back to Jones, who was once more staring out of the window through blank eyes.

'Can we ask you about the book David Stabler was writing about you?' asked Harris.

'I don't read books. I read magazines about animals. I like animals.' Jones pointed to the courtyard and smiled brightly. 'You get all sorts of birds out there, you know. And sometimes you get a squirrel. I like it when that happens. I like squirrels.'

'I'm sure you do,' said Harris. His voice was soft. Gentle. 'Did Mr Stabler come to visit you?'

Jones thought for a few moments.

'There was a man taking photographs of animals. He had a camera.' Jones gave another smile. 'I like animals.'

Harris glanced at Gallagher, who shrugged.

'Been there, got the T-shirt,' said the sergeant.

Harris nodded and turned back to the old man.

'Did you meet him?' asked the inspector. 'This man with the camera?'

'I didn't meet anyone,' said Jones. 'Not until I came here. I was surprised. I thought I was the last man alive.'

'In some ways you are,' said Harris. 'Tell me, have you met anyone from Germany? Josef Haller, perhaps?'

'I don't know anyone from Germany. I've been in China.' Jones fixed the inspector with a hard look and there was a fierce glint in his eye that defied disagreement. 'I told you that. I've been in China.'

'Of course,' said Harris. He held up his hands in surrender. 'My mistake, for which I apologise, Simon.'

'I'm George. George Garvie.' The old man looked at Gallagher. 'Why does he not listen?'

'I am sure that he's sorry,' said the sergeant. 'We just need to know if you…'

Jones shook his head vigorously and turned away from the detectives to resume his perusal of the courtyard. Harris glanced at the nurse, who shook her head.

'That's the best you'll get out of him,' she said. 'He gets very angry if you disagree with him and he'll not talk to you now. I really think it would be best if you left.'

Harris nodded and stood up.

'Thank you for your time, Mr Jones,' he said.

'Rider,' said the old man without turning back to his visitors. 'My name's Matthew Rider.'

Harris looked quizzically at his sergeant.

'Another of the names he used at Hillview Cottage,' said Gallagher.

'He's given us half a dozen,' said the nurse. She gestured towards the door. 'Please, gentlemen. I think that we need to leave him to rest now.'

Harris nodded and turned back to the old man.

'Good day, Mr Rider,' he said. 'Thank you for your help.'

Simon Jones did not reply but kept staring through the window at the birds. The police officers followed the nurse out of the room.

'As you can see,' she said as they started to walk down the corridor, 'his mind's pretty much gone. Reality and imagination get all mixed up.'

'I don't suppose there's any chance that he could be faking it, is there?' asked Harris.

The nurse looked surprised.

'Why on earth would you think that?' she asked.

'There was a suggestion at one point,' explained Harris. 'To evade the police.'

'Does it look like it's faked?' The nurse looked at Gallagher. 'You'll know if your father went through it.'

'It rang horribly true to me,' said Gallagher.

'Why are you interested in him anyway?' asked the nurse. 'What's he supposed to have done?'

'Just at the moment,' said Harris as she led them into the reception area, 'I'm not entirely sure.'

The detectives had just left Barry Gordon and walked back to the Land Rover when Harris's mobile phone rang.

The inspector unlocked the doors and once they were in the vehicle, he put the device on speaker so that Gallagher could hear.

'Gillian,' said the inspector. 'I take it you have news?'

'Do I.' Roberts sounded excited; it was not something they were used to experiencing with the level-headed detective inspector. 'I've just come off the phone from Dusseldorf.'

'And?' said Harris.

'You are right.'

'Let's take that as a given, shall we? However, maybe you would like to enlighten me about what I know?'

'You said that Josef Haller might be lying,' said Roberts. 'See, I talked to the local commander. I told you that we should have done it earlier. He was reluctant to talk to me at first – wanted to speak to you as the senior officer – but the more I told him the more co-operative he became. He had no idea about what's been happening.'

'And what *has* been happening?' asked Harris.

'Haller's been quite clever, actually. There's enough about his story to give it the ring of truth were we ever to start asking questions. For starters, he *is* an intelligence officer and he does have high-level security clearance. However, he doesn't deal with terrorism. He's a largely desk-bound officer handling more routine information. He's red hot on technology, though, and he could easily have installed that alert on the fingerprint record himself. The commander certainly knew nothing about it.'

'And the armed robberies that he claims the gang has been carrying out?' asked Harris.

'Again, there's a ring of truth,' said Roberts. 'There *have* been some robberies in the area over recent months but the commander said that they arrested a local bunch for them a couple of weeks ago and there's nothing to link them with terrorists.'

'Did you mention Thomas Haller?'

'I did, yes, and the commander confirmed that Josef is his son. Thomas is in his seventies now and in poor health. The commander does not know him personally and events in 1984 were before his time but he did confirm what your chap told you in Manchester last night, that there were rumours surrounding the police team.'

'What kind of rumours?' asked Harris.

'Suggestions that someone fed information about the prison van's route before the break-out. There was some kind of internal inquiry to see if any of the detectives leaked the information but it doesn't sound like it was very thorough and the unit was cleared of any wrongdoing, including Thomas Haller.'

'Interesting,' said Harris. 'But it doesn't give us anything to connect Josef to the murders, does it? Presumably he was in Germany when Stabler and Cronin were killed. He had to fly in for today's meeting at headquarters.'

'Maybe that's what he *told* you.' Roberts could not keep the sense of triumph out of her voice. 'According to the commander, Haller has not been at work for the past ten days. Sick leave. He told his boss it was an injury sustained in a five-a-side football match. I had folks checking flights in and out of Dusseldorf and he was not booked on any of them.'

'Even more interesting,' said Harris.

'And I've not finished,' said Roberts. The detectives could tell that she was enjoying herself. 'Geoff Smith has been on from North Yorkshire. They have come up with a report of a car spotted near the cottage at the time that Cronin was shot. Turns out to be a rental vehicle hired at Manchester Airport just over a week ago by a man who gave a different name to Haller but had a slight German accent. I've got an alert out with strict instructions that it isn't stopped until we say so.'

'And I knew all this, did I?' said Harris. 'Boy, I'm good.'

'You must be. What do you want to do next? We need to move fast before Josef works out that we are onto him.'

'Is the German commander happy for us to handle it?'

'I'm not sure happy is the word but yes. And he's promised to keep it to himself in case any of Haller's colleagues are in on it.'

'I doubt they are, he sounds like a lone wolf to me,' said Harris. 'That's brilliant work, Gillian. I'll have a think and ring you back in a few minutes. Listen, make sure that the team keep this to themselves, will you? I don't want anyone finding out, particularly not Special Branch. I don't want to risk anything getting back to Haller. There's too much being leaked, for my liking.'

'Understood,' said Roberts. This time, she did not object to keeping information away from colleagues.

Harris ended the call and looked at Gallagher.

'But why would Haller go to all that trouble?' asked the sergeant.

'Presumably, because his father was involved in the prison van incident somehow. Maybe Josef is worried that, if Simon Jones is caught, it will all come out and that his father could end up in prison. Gillian said he was in poor health, remember.'

Gallagher thought of his own frail father in his final months.

'Which of us wouldn't want to protect our fathers?' he said. 'I certainly would.'

'But, surely, you wouldn't kill to do it?'

Gallagher shrugged.

'Who knows how any of us would react until it happens to us?' he said.

'You know,' said Harris. He glanced back towards the nursing home. 'One thing's certain, though, Josef Haller would appear not to know that Simon Jones's dementia is real. We can use that.'

The inspector noticed that Barry Gordon was still standing next to his vehicle, deep in conversation on his mobile phone. Harris got out of the Land Rover and walked over to him. The constable ended his call.

'My governor,' he explained. 'She wants to know what's happening.'

'Who else in your team knows the true story behind what's going on here?' asked Harris.

'No one, as far as I know. Just me and my governor. To everyone else, he's just another old man with dementia. Who else would care?'

'Indeed,' said Harris. 'Would it be possible to have this place watched round the clock, do you think? Starting now? Just for twenty-four hours?'

'I guess,' said Gordon. His eyes gleamed at the thought of being further involved in a major murder inquiry. 'I'd certainly be happy to do some of it if my governor agreed. What are you thinking?'

'I am wondering how she is when it comes to thinking outside the box?'

Gordon looked bewildered.

'Outside the box?' he asked.

Harris nodded.

'Well outside the box,' he said.

The inspector gave a slight smile and phoned the Special Branch office at headquarters. It was Bourne who answered.

'Charlie,' said the inspector. 'Jack Harris. Your governor not around?'

'Sorry, Jack, she's in meetings for the rest of the day and can't be disturbed.'

'I need to see her.'

'It's not exactly convenient,' said Bourne.

'Then might I suggest that you make it convenient,' said Harris.

Bourne recalled using the same words to the inspector and sighed, sensing that the rules of the game had changed.

'I'll see what I can do,' he said.

# Chapter twenty-seven

Harris and Gallagher arrived at force headquarters later that afternoon and headed for the chief constable's office. Half an hour later, they walked into Janet Maynard's room, where she was waiting for them with Charlie Bourne. Both looked concerned.

'This had better be good, Jack,' said Maynard, dispensing with civilities as the detectives walked into her office without knocking. 'I thought we'd straightened all this out.'

'New rules,' said Harris, sitting down. 'This time we play the game my way.'

'I'm really not in the mood to–'

'Then perhaps you're in the mood to explain to the chief constable why your department has been assisting a man suspected of committing a double murder, instead,' said Harris. 'Hardly the ideal start to your time with us, might I suggest.'

Maynard appeared as if she was about to protest but something about the look on the inspector's face persuaded her to keep silent and she and Bourne sat and listened in mounting consternation as Harris outlined how he proposed to bring the investigation to a close.

'I'm not sure about this,' said Maynard. 'Even assuming that you're right and I remain to–'

'Oh, we're right,' said Gallagher. It was the first time he had spoken since entering the room. 'Our team has been checking back through ANPR and can place Haller's rented car near both murder scenes. What's more, he didn't catch the plane after this morning's meeting – he booked into a bed and breakfast near Carlisle instead. My guess is that he'll ring Charlie before the day is out to see if he can't point him in the direction of Simon Jones.'

'He already has,' said Bourne gloomily.

'There you are then,' said Harris. 'Face it, guys, we've been played.'

'So, it would seem,' said Maynard. She was silent for a few moments as she considered the ramifications of what she was being told. None of them were good. 'However, I'm still not convinced that this is the way to go about things. Why don't you just pick him up since you know where he is?'

'Because everything we have on him is circumstantial. A good lawyer would punch holes in it. No, we need to catch him in the act, to be sure.'

'I need some time to–' began Maynard.

'We don't have time,' said Harris. 'If he works out that we're onto him, we'll lose him. And the Preston cops are happy enough to play along.'

Still Maynard shook her head.

'I'm sorry, Jack,' she said. 'It's a no go. Not until I've had chance to–'

'I guess Geoff Smith was right,' said Harris in an off-hand way. He glanced at Gallagher. 'Eh, Matty lad?'

'I guess so,' said the sergeant. 'Pity. You'd rather prefer someone with his outdated opinions to be wrong.'

Maynard gave him a sharp look.

'Geoff Smith?' she said. 'At North Yorkshire? Why have you been talking to him?'

'He's leading the investigation into James Cronin's murder,' said Harris.

'And what did he say about me?' she said bleakly. 'As if I didn't know?'

'He reckons that you have no imagination,' said Harris. 'He said you're too straight-laced to make a success of a job like Special Branch.'

Maynard gave Harris a knowing look.

'Now who's playing me?' she said. She chewed her lip angrily. 'But I'll go along with it. The man has never liked me. He doesn't like seeing any woman landing top jobs. Well, being played or not, I'm not about to let someone like Geoff Smith get away with saying things like that.'

Harris looked at Gallagher.

'I guess Geoff Smith was wrong about her, after all,' he said.

Gallagher nodded.

'So, it would seem,' he said. 'I thought he might be.'

'But before you go ahead, I still have to check with the chief constable,' cautioned Maynard. 'I'm sure you can appreciate that I can't just go ahead with something like this on my own authority.'

'By all means check,' said Harris. 'But we've just come from him and he's sanctioned everything.'

Maynard thought for a few moments then nodded.

'So, what exactly do you need us to do?' she asked.

'We want you to set a little trap,' said Harris.

* * *

Twenty minutes later, Harris and Gallagher had only just left the meeting to return to Preston when Bourne's mobile phone rang. He glanced at the read-out then at Maynard.

'Haller,' he said. 'What do you want me to do?'

'Exactly what Jack asked you to do. Like he says, we're playing by his rules now.'

'Are you sure? I mean, *really* sure? If it goes wrong…'

'I'm sure. Do it.'

Bourne shrugged and took the call.

'Josef,' he said. 'I was just about to ring you. Harris and his team have arrested Simon Jones in Preston. He wasn't going to tell you but I felt that you should know.'

'I appreciate the gesture, Charlie,' said Haller. 'But I thought that Harris had agreed to do as he was told.'

'Yeah, but he's an obstinate so-and-so and he's gone over my governor's head.' He glanced at Maynard, who nodded. 'She's furious about it but the chief constable has come down on Harris's side and given him permission to interview Jones about the murders.'

'And will he talk, do you know?' asked Haller.

'It would seem so. From what I'm hearing, he's sick of living life on the run. Says he wants to make a statement. Have everything out in the open.'

'Have they interviewed him yet?'

'Not yet. But they will.'

'How do you know all this?' asked Haller.

Bourne could sense that the German was worried. Even though he was trying to convey an air of calm, the anxiety came through in his voice.

'A mate of mine works on his team and thinks that Harris is acting too high-handed,' said Bourne. 'Doesn't like the idea of his governor doing something that could allow terrorists to escape. He reckons that Harris never had any intention of abiding by your agreement. Wants all the glory for himself. He's like that.'

'When's he going to do the interview?'

'Tomorrow morning.'

'Why are they leaving it so long?' asked Haller suspiciously.

'Jones hurt his leg while trying to escape. Nothing serious but he's had to go hospital for treatment so they've decided to hold him in Preston overnight and bring him north first thing in the morning.'

‘Do you know when?’ asked Haller. ‘And what they’ll be driving?’

‘Why do you want to know? What are you planning to do?’

‘There’s no way I can let Harris get away with this,’ said Haller. ‘There’s too much at stake. If I’m going to pull some strings at this end, it would be helpful if I knew their planned movements for tomorrow.’

‘From what I’ve been told, he’s due to leave at 7:30am. They’ll be in a black Audi. Listen, Josef, if Harris starts asking where the information came from…’

‘Don’t worry, Charlie,’ said Haller. ‘I’ll keep you well out of it. If he does start asking questions, just say it’s down to national security and that you had no option but to co-operate with us.’

‘I’m not going to say anything to Jack Harris, believe me,’ said Bourne. ‘If he finds out that I’ve blown his plan he’ll be furious. He’s perfectly capable of beating the living daylights out of me.’

‘You worry too much,’ said Haller. ‘Text me the exact details of the police station, will you, for the sat nav?’

‘Sure.’

When the call had ended, Bourne placed his mobile on the desk and looked at Maynard.

‘I feel sick,’ he said.

# Chapter twenty-eight

Harris and Gallagher exchanged nervous glances as, just before 7:30am the following morning, they walked out of the rear exit of the police station in Preston. After glancing round once more, they crossed the yard in the direction of a black Audi with tinted rear windows, which had been borrowed from the local undercover surveillance unit. Both detectives wore sidearms and Kevlar vests and were trying to give each other the impression that they were not worried as they climbed into the vehicle.

'Right then,' said Gallagher.

Harris nodded and started up the engine. As he did so, the radio crackled into life. It was one of the firearms team who was sitting in an unmarked vehicle parked close to the police station.

'We've got a blue BMW approaching,' said a man's voice. 'It's coming up on our records as the rental vehicle that chummy is supposed to be driving.'

'Keep your distance,' said Harris.

'Affirmative,' said the firearms officer and the airwaves went quiet again.

'He's going to go through with it then,' said Gallagher. He glanced across at Harris. 'I was rather hoping that we were wrong.'

'So was I,' said Harris.

The inspector edged the Audi out of the yard and into the early morning traffic. Gallagher glanced into his side-mirror and saw the BMW come into view and slot into the flow of cars behind them. Gallagher shook his head.

'He must be desperate to try something this risky,' he said.

'He's gone too far, hasn't he? He has to finish what he started.' Harris looked in his rear-view mirror at the BMW. 'He's in far too deep to do anything else.'

'I guess.'

'Besides, he has no idea that we're onto him. I'm not sure that he'd be here if he did. He'd be putting as much distance between us and him as possible.'

'Now there's a nice idea,' said Gallagher. 'I'll think about that instead.'

The firearms officer's low voice crackled over the radio airwaves again.

'I take it that you've clocked him?' he said.

'Yeah, we see him,' said Harris.

'Remember what we said. When he gets close, we're deploying. This is our show and we don't want any heroics.'

'Understood,' said Harris.

'Yes, well, just make sure it *is* understood,' said the firearms officer sternly. 'You've got a reputation.'

'Yeah,' said Gallagher with a slight smile as he glanced at his boss. 'This isn't London, you know. You can't come to a place like this with your woolyback ways.'

Harris gave a low laugh and guided the Audi through the traffic and onto the outskirts of the city, heading in the direction of the junction which would take them onto the northbound M6. As the vehicles left the built-up area behind and the traffic momentarily thinned out, Gallagher glanced in the side-view mirror again.

'I'd try it here if I was him,' he said.

'Me, too,' said Harris.

As he did so, the BMW driver jammed his foot onto the accelerator and smoothly overtook two vehicles and slotted in directly behind the Audi.

'Here we go,' said Harris.

Gallagher said nothing but was acutely aware of the pounding of his heart and the sweat glistening on his brow. He noticed that his leg was trembling.

'You'll learn to appreciate the quiet life,' he muttered. 'That's what Julie said when she persuaded me to move up north. Quiet life, my arse!'

The BMW driver continued to follow them for a few more seconds before making his move as the detectives passed a road sign indicating that the motorway was only a couple of miles away. With a sudden squeal of tyres, the BMW overtook the Audi at speed and, with a yank of the steering wheel, the driver sent his vehicle slewing to a juddering halt, forcing Harris to slam down hard on the Audi's brakes and bring his vehicle to a sudden stop. It was all over in seconds. A masked man leapt out of the BMW's driver's seat, brandishing a handgun at the Audi, but before Harris and Gallagher could react, two dark-coloured saloon cars screeched to a halt and several police firearms officers jumped out. The air was filled with hollered warnings as they trained their guns on the startled gunman.

'Drop your weapon!'

'On the ground!'

'Arms outstretched where we can see your hands!'

The gunman hesitated for a moment.

'Don't be a hero!' shouted one of the firearms officers. 'Drop your weapon or we will fire!'

Still the gunman hesitated but, just as it appeared that he was prepared to ignore the order, he saw Harris getting out of the Audi, nodded his head in defeat, dropped his weapon with a clatter of gunmetal on tarmac and lay on the ground with his arms outstretched. Harris ran over to where the armed officers were bringing the situation under control. One of them handcuffed the shocked gunman and hauled him roughly to his feet. Harris nodded at the firearms officers.

'Good work, lads,' he said. 'Textbook.'

The inspector reached over and removed the balaclava to reveal the ashen face staring back at him through wide eyes.

'Josef Haller,' he said. 'I am arresting you on suspicion of the murders of David Stabler and James Cronin.'

'How did you know it was me?' gasped Haller.

Harris glanced at Gallagher.

'It's a father thing,' he said.

Gallagher nodded his appreciation at the comment and looked at the handgun on the ground then at the abject figure of Josef Haller. He thought of his father.

'You're right,' said the sergeant. He looked at Harris. 'I *do* know which side of the law I would come down on.'

Harris reached out and patted him gently on the shoulder.

'Of course, you do,' he said.

## Chapter twenty-nine

Gallagher walked into Jack Harris's office shortly after 3:30pm to find the inspector staring intently at the computer screen. He had spent several hours speed-reading the most up-to-date version of the book that had been found on James Cronin's laptop and seized from Josef Haller following his arrest that morning.

'Quite a story,' said Harris, looking up.

'Makes for good reading, doesn't it?' replied Gallagher. He sat down at the desk. 'No wonder Heather Murrell was prepared to spend all that money on it. It could be a real blockbuster. People love true crime.'

'It's certainly quite a tale,' said Harris. The inspector sat back and rubbed eyes that had grown weary after so many hours of non-stop reading. 'Did you see the briefing note that Stabler wrote for Cronin?'

'Yeah, I did. Seems that Stabler was working on a feature on something else for a German magazine when someone told him about Simon Jones. He'd never heard of the guy but, once he found out that he had been largely forgotten, he had the idea for the book. I'm assuming the suggestion that the police organised his escape from the prison van was the new angle that Stabler was trying to confirm?'

'I think it must have been,' said Harris.

'He couldn't really ignore it, could he? Bent cops may leave a sour taste in the mouth, but they make for a good story, don't they?'

'I am afraid they do.' Harris tapped his computer screen. 'But Thomas Haller refused to speak to Stabler so he was hoping that Simon Jones would confirm the story. Trouble was, Jones had dementia. If Stabler knew that, he didn't tell anyone. Maybe he found out the day he was murdered. Didn't have a chance to tell anyone.'

'Even if he did already know, would you let on?' said Gallagher. 'I mean, if Heather Murrell thought that the big scoop was a bloke who only has eyes for squirrels, she'd probably have demanded her money back.'

'I guess.' Harris stood up. 'Come on, let's have a chat with our Mr Haller. We've left him to stew long enough, I think.'

A few minutes later, the detectives were sitting in an interview room, staring across the desk at the cowed figure of Josef Haller. The confidence that the German had displayed during the meeting in the Special Branch offices the previous day had gone and he sat with his shoulders hunched and his eyes staring at the floor. His lawyer eyed her client with concern.

'Has he been checked out by a doctor?' she asked.

'He has,' said Harris. 'He says that Mr Haller is well enough to be interviewed.'

The lawyer looked doubtful but did not say anything. Harris turned his attention to Haller.

'So, Josef,' he said, 'your father was a corrupt policeman, then. How much was he paid to let Simon Jones escape?'

Fire flashed in Haller's eyes.

'No!' he exclaimed. He leapt to his feet. 'It wasn't like that!'

'Sit down!' rasped Harris.

Haller glared at him.

'Sit down!' repeated Harris.

Haller hesitated then did as he was told.

'But it's not what you think,' he said.

'Well, what is it?' asked Harris. 'David Stabler seemed pretty convinced that he helped organise Simon Jones's escape from the prison van. As he says in the book, the only possible explanation is that he and the others did it for money.'

'Well, that's not true.'

'Then enlighten us,' said the inspector. 'If they didn't do it for money, why did they do it?'

Haller sighed.

'It was Schulz's idea,' he said. 'Neumann went along with it – reluctantly, I think. My father did not want anything to do with it but Schulz forced him. He was like you, a big man, and he could be intimidating, especially for younger officers. And he was my father's boss. But it wasn't for money. None of them were corrupt.'

'So why do it?' asked Harris. 'Why do something that risky?'

'You must believe me when I say that they acted out of the best of intentions,' replied Haller. 'You see, after his arrest, Simon Jones told them that he would be prepared to act as an informant and give them what they needed to put the whole gang away. Schulz knew that the evidence they had was not particularly strong – no one was prepared to stand up in court and give evidence – and the last thing any of them wanted after almost a year of investigation was for the case to collapse. They had too much riding on it. Put them behind bars and careers would be made, watch it fail and they'd be unlikely to get promotions in the future. There was a lot at stake. Schulz agreed to work with Jones and persuaded the others.'

'And what did Jones get out of it?' asked Gallagher.

'Immunity from prosecution and a new identity. The trouble was, he said that he didn't want it to look like he was helping the police and insisted on the prison break-out to make it look like criminals were involved. He said there'd be less chance of retribution against him that way.' Haller shook his head. 'But the whole thing was a set-up. He had no intention of helping the police. All he was interested in was getting away.'

'The book says that Neumann drove the car and your father was the gunman,' said Harris.

'That's right, yes. Schulz handled things at the police station, made sure that Jones got into the right van. The agreement was that after they'd stopped the van, Jones would get into the car and they'd get him out of the city.'

'But it went wrong,' said the inspector.

'Badly wrong,' said Haller. He shook his head again. 'Not only did they not realise until it was too late that Jones had betrayed them, but they hadn't bargained on the prison guard trying to be a hero.'

'So, your father shot him?'

Haller took a few moments to compose his thoughts, battling strong emotions.

'Yes, but not deliberately,' he said eventually. 'He panicked.'

'The book claims that it was deliberate,' said Harris.

'Yes, well that's not true,' replied Haller. The fire was back in his eyes. 'My father is not a murderer, Chief Inspector. It was an accident. He was not accustomed to handling firearms and pulled the trigger by mistake. Not that anyone would believe it. That's why I had to stop the story coming out. There was no way I was going to allow my father to die in prison. He deserves better than that.'

'But you didn't mind other people dying, did you?' said Gallagher. He was unable to conceal his distaste for what he was hearing. 'Stabler and Cronin, for a start. And you were perfectly prepared to shoot Simon Jones this morning.'

'It's a question of priorities, Sergeant.' Haller looked at him. 'Surely, you can understand that? We'd do anything for our fathers, wouldn't we?'

Gallagher glanced at Harris.

'Yes, but we wouldn't kill for them,' he said.

Harris gave the sergeant a slight nod then turned back to Haller.

'And Jones?' he asked. 'What happened to him after the getaway?'

'Vanished into thin air.'

'People don't just vanish into thin air,' said Harris.

'Well, Simon Jones did. There were questions at the time, of course, but nothing was ever proved – how could it be? Jones was the only one who could point the finger at my father and the others and he wasn't going to come forward. Besides, a couple of other gang members turned informant and they got the convictions anyway. In time, everyone forgot about what had happened.'

'I'm sure the prison guard's family didn't,' said Gallagher.

Haller said nothing.

'Then along comes David Stabler?' said Harris. 'An investigative journalist with an obsession for the truth and a book to write.'

'I'd heard rumours but, at first, I was not worried,' said Haller. 'He'd been talking to a couple of underworld figures and a couple of former police officers but nothing I was hearing suggested that he knew about my father's involvement and, even if he did, Schulz and Neumann were dead, leaving my father and Jones as the only ones who could confirm it – I was pretty sure they couldn't publish the book without at least one of them. My father wasn't going to say anything and Jones had been missing for the best part of forty years. I didn't even know if he was still alive. Without talking to him, all Stabler had was unsubstantiated hearsay.'

'Did he contact your father?' asked Harris.

'He did but my father put the phone down on him. He tried a couple more times but my father put the phone down again and eventually he stopped trying. Then I heard that Stabler was close to finding Jones. I knew that if Jones talked, it would all come out. My father was terrified and asked me to make sure that he didn't. I'd never seen him in tears before but he was that day.' Haller gave them a hopeless look. 'How could I refuse him? I mean, what would you have done?'

Gallagher said nothing.

'How did you track Stabler down?' asked Harris.

'It's not difficult if you know where to look, particularly with my level of security clearance.'

'But why kill him?' asked the inspector.

'It was an accident.' Haller shook his head. 'If he'd been sensible about it, we could have come to some sort of agreement and he'd still be alive today but he tried to grab the gun and it went off.'

'The Hallers seem to have a poor record when it comes to guns going off,' said the inspector.

Haller gave him a bleak look but said nothing.

'What did you do next?' asked Harris.

'Once I read Stabler's notes, I knew that Jones was at Hillview Cottage. The trouble was that the storm had closed in and I had to sit out the night in the tent.'

'With the body?' asked Harris.

'Yes, with the body.' Haller shuddered at the memory. 'I was terrified that a hiker or someone like that would stumble upon us, but no one came. Next morning, I set fire to Stabler's car so you would struggle to identify him and make the link with Jones, and headed for the cottage.'

'To kill him?'

'If necessary, although I rather hoped that Stabler's death would convince him to stay quiet, or retract anything that he might have said. I could not believe it when I saw police officers there. A burglary, wasn't it?'

'It was,' said Harris. 'We caught the guy with the television as he tried to leave the area. Your family seems to suffer from a lot of bad luck, Josef. I assume it was you who set up the alert on the fingerprint database?'

'A few weeks previously, yes. When it went off, I knew that it was only a matter of time before you made the connection.'

'So, you made up a bogus story about terrorists and roped Special Branch into it?' said Harris.

'It wasn't difficult.' Haller gave a slight smile. 'They were very trusting. You English do have a singular belief in fair play, I must say. *You* were the problem. I didn't trust you at all.'

'I'll take that as a compliment. What about James Cronin? How did you find him?'

'Stabler had left a note with his details so I rang him up and told him I was prepared to co-operate with the book. When he tried to get out of the cottage, I had no alternative but to kill him.'

'There's always an alternative,' said Harris.

'Not for me, there wasn't, Chief Inspector. Anyway, the rest you know. I take it that Jones has given you a statement implicating my father?'

'Well, there's the irony of it,' said Harris. He sat back in his chair and gave a slight smile. 'You see, it turns out that he wasn't pretending to have dementia. As far as he was concerned, he really was the last man alive.'

Josef Haller closed his eyes.

# Epilogue

Six months later, three weeks after Josef Haller had admitted murder and been jailed for life, Jack Harris sat in his office and started to read the email that had been sent early that morning. He didn't really need to read the message from the manager of the nursing home in Preston, he could guess what it said. "Dear Mr Harris," began the message, "I have to regretfully inform you that…"

The inspector's desk phone rang and he stopped reading and picked up the receiver.

'Harris,' he said.

'It's Gina,' said the press officer.

'Just the person.' Harris returned his attention to the email. 'Can you prepare that press release we talked about, please?'

'Simon Jones has died then?'

'Yeah, last night.' The inspector rang a finger down the screen. 'You can attribute it to pneumonia, if you want. Keep it short, yeah? And no quote from me. I'm not sure what I could say anyway.'

'Will do,' said Jeffers. 'I'm actually ringing because I've just had Chris Steward on from *The Organisation.* He wants to talk to you.'

'Well, tell him that I don't want to talk to him.'

'He's most insistent. Says that it won't take long and that it could be to your advantage.'

'That'll be the day,' said Harris.

'Will you ring him?'

'I don't really think…'

'Pretty please? It's a respected magazine and it could do the force some good to feature in it from time to time. At least ask him what he wants? He said he'd rather discuss it directly with you.'

Harris sighed.

'Very well,' he said. 'But only because it's you, Gina.'

'Thanks, Jack,' she said. 'Much appreciated.'

After they ended their conversation, Harris was about to call Chris Steward when Gillian Roberts walked into the office.

'Can you talk?' she asked. She gestured to the mobile phone in his hand. 'I can always come back.'

'No, it's nothing important. What are you after?'

'I've just had my friendly German police commander on. He thought we would like to know that their prosecutors have decided not to press ahead with the court case against Thomas Haller on health grounds. Not in the public interest etc.'

'I'm not really surprised. He doesn't sound like he's long for this world. Looks like Josef did it all for nothing.' Harris reached for the document that lay on top of the pile of papers in his in-tray. 'Talking of Josef, we've just heard that the application from his lawyers for him to be transferred to a German prison so that he can see his father has been granted. And on the subject of the old and frail, Simon Jones died last night.'

'Did the home manage to track down any relatives?'

'Not a single one,' said Harris. 'He died like he lived, alone. The duty nurse checked in on him just after three and he'd stopped breathing.'

'And there goes the last man alive,' said Roberts. She shook her head. 'A sad business all round.'

'Indeed,' said Harris.

Once the detective inspector had gone, he returned to making his call to Chris Steward.

'Jack?' said the publisher's voice. 'Thanks for ringing back.'

'That's Detective Chief Inspector Harris to you.'

'Oh, come on, don't be like that.'

'How do you expect me to react?' said Harris. 'I asked you to keep our conversation about David Stabler to yourself then you went and told *The Daily News*.'

'Would it make a difference if I said that I wasn't the one who did that?'

'No, it wouldn't,' replied Harris. 'Anyway, I've said my piece. What do you want?'

'Heather Murrell has sent me a review copy of the book. One of their writers finished it off and they're bringing it out now that Josef Haller has been jailed. They've called it *The Last Man Alive*.'

Harris glanced back at the email from the manager of the nursing home.

'There's nothing like a touch of irony,' he said.

'What does that mean?'

'Nothing,' said Harris. 'What has all this got to do with me?'

'Well, it's going to be a big story. According to Heather Murrell, she's in the final stages of agreeing a serialisation deal with a national newspaper and there's talk of a Netflix film as well.'

'So?'

'So, you come out of the book very well,' said Steward. 'A somewhat heroic character, one might even say. Who knows, maybe they can get someone like Chris Hemsworth to play you in the movie?'

'Who?'

'Chris Hemsworth. Thor?'

Harris was silent.

'Never mind,' said Steward. 'Anyway, I wondered if, what with all the interest that there's going to be, you might like to reconsider and do an interview for my magazine?'

'I told you my answer last time.'

'Yes, I know,' said Steward. 'But I thought you might think again. In memory of the two lads who died, if for no other reason?'

Harris considered the request for a few moments.

'No,' he said.

And he put the phone down.

THE END

## List of characters

*Levton Bridge Police:*

Superintendent Philip Curtis – divisional commander
Detective Chief Inspector Jack Harris – head of divisional CID
Detective Inspector Gillian Roberts
Detective Sergeant Matty Gallagher
Detective Constable Alison Butterfield
Detective Constable Alistair Marshall
Detective Constable Sally Orr
Kevin Guthrie – forensics officer
Mary Josephs – forensics officer

*County Police Force:*

Detective Chief Inspector Janet Maynard – Head of Special Branch
Detective Sergeant Charlie Bourne – Special Branch
Gina Jeffers – force press officer

*Other police service personnel:*

Michael Fischer – retired German police officer

Constable Barry Gordon – Lancashire Constabulary
Josef Haller – intelligence officer with the German Police
Thomas Haller – his father, retired German police officer
Graham Leckie – intelligence officer with Greater Manchester Police
Detective Constable Danny Mahler – Metropolitan police officer
Walter Neumann – former German police officer
Mark Ramage – works for the National Police Air Service (NPAS)
Ernest Schulz – former German police officer
Detective Chief Inspector Geoff Smith – North Yorkshire police officer

*Other characters:*

James Cronin – freelance journalist and author
Bob Crowther – Head of Levton Bridge Mountain Rescue Team
Doc – Home Office pathologist
Mike Ganton – Deputy Head of Levton Bridge Mountain Rescue Team
Francis Jacques aka Midas – London gangland figure
Julie Gallagher – Matty Gallagher's wife, nurse at Roxham General Hospital
Lee Garritt – London-based gang member
Miranda Hayes – PA at Sudden Death Books
Simon Jones – pensioner
Tommy Lacey – burglar
Heather Murrell – publisher at Sudden Death Books
Professor Neal Radcliffe – psychiatrist at Roxham General Hospital
Max Rodney – London-based gang member
Geoff Riley – property landlord
Mally Ross – delivery driver
Jeremy Rowley – London-based solicitor
David Stabler – freelance journalist and author

Margie Stabler – David's mother
Chris Steward – publisher of *The Organisation* magazine

If you enjoyed this book, please let others know by leaving a quick review on Amazon. Also, if you spot anything untoward in the paperback, get in touch. We strive for the best quality and appreciate reader feedback.

editor@thebookfolks.com

www.thebookfolks.com

## ALSO BY JOHN DEAN

*In this series:*

Dead Hill (Book 1)
The Vixen's Scream (Book 2)
To Die Alone (Book 3)
To Honour the Dead (Book 4)
Thou Shalt Kill (Book 5)
Error of Judgement (Book 6)
The Killing Line (Book 7)
Kill Shot (Book 8)
The Girl in the Meadow (Book 10)
To Catch a Lie (Book 11)

*In the DCI John Blizzard series:*

The Long Dead
Strange Little Girl
The Railway Man
The Secrets Man
A Breach of Trust
Death List
A Flicker in the Night
The Latch Man
No Age to Die
The Vengeance Man
The Name on the Bullet

**DISCOVER JOHN DEAN'S DCI JOHN BLIZZARD SERIES**

All books FREE with Kindle Unlimited and available in paperback.

Printed in Dunstable, United Kingdom

68045312R00112